Caeia March was born in the I   : M in in 194   und grew up in industrial South York are. She went to London University in 1964, graduated in social sciences and went on to be a tutor of women's studies and creative writing. She left London in 1990 and settled in the far west of Cornwall, where she co-founded the West Cornwall Women's Land Trust – a tree planting and conservation project for women. She has published poetry, short stories and non-fiction articles, but is best known for her much-loved novels, all published by The Women's Press: *Three Ply Yarn* (1986), *The Hide and Seek Files* (1988), *Fire! Fire!* (1991), *Reflections* (1995), *Between the Worlds* (1996) and *Spinsters' Rock* (1999). She is also the editor of *Knowing ME* (1998).

Caeia March has two sons, ages twenty-eight and thirty, and she now lives with her life-partner, Cynth Morris, in Devon where they are creating two beautiful allotment gardens on a hillside overlooking Dartmoor.

Also by Caeia March from The Women's Press:

Long Journey Home

Short Stories by New Lesbian Writers

CAEIA MARCH, EDITOR

First published by The Women's Press Ltd, 2001
A member of the Namara Group
34 Great Sutton Street, London EC1V OLQ
www.the-womens-press.com

Collection copyright © Caeia March 2001

'Tzimmes' is an extract from *Tzimmes,* book twenty-seven in the a+bend press small book series, San Francisco, May 2000.

British Library Cataloguing-in-Publication Data
A catalogue record for this book is available from the British Library.

ISBN 0 7043 4575 7

Typeset by FiSH Books Ltd, London WC1
Printed and bound in Great Britain by CPD (Wales) Ltd, Ebbw Vale

Contents

Introduction

I approached The Women's Press in 1997 with the idea for this rich and diverse anthology because I felt that I was in a unique position from which to encourage new lesbian writing. I wanted to create a dynamic collection, showing lesbian life as we know it today. My main focus would be multi-racial Britain, set within an international framework because we have lesbian connections, friends, relations, children and lovers all over the world. I wanted fabulous writing and a celebration of our zany individuality because we are funny and strong as well as ordinary, weird and wonderful. Lesbians do it all sorts of ways – and we are, quite simply, everywhere.

There is no one way to be a lesbian, to live or work or experience our sexuality, so my in-house editors agreed with me that we wanted new writers who would express a wide variety of feelings, lifestyles and ways of being. I wanted stories that told quietly, insistently, of the warmth of woman-loving and I also wanted to be authentic – revealing the variety of ways that lesbians experience displacement, or learn to overcome loneliness, separation, grief and loss.

I was touched by the honesty, vulnerability and beauty of many of the submitted pieces, including fifty 'coming out' stories which we decided not to include when we chose to focus predominantly upon the lives of lesbians who were already 'out and proud'. I am very grateful for the opportunity to read all the submitted stories, and would like to acknowledge the skill and craftswomanship of the writers, and the strength and humour of the lesbians represented in their writings.

However it was also chillingly obvious through the submissions that many adult lesbians – alongside our heterosexual sisters – have spent years overcoming their childhood terror of abuse by fathers, uncles, brothers and grandfathers. Several of those early submissions were entitled 'Coming Home'.

Steadily the title and coherence of the collection began to emerge. I had been involved for many years in straight socialist-feminist and anti-racist politics in the seventies, before my own 'coming out' in 1980 – therefore on my bookshelf, sitting next to Steve Biko's *I Write What I Like*, has been a short story collection by a Black male writer named Julius Lester entitled *Long Journey Home* (Longman – Knockouts, 1977), which was both an inspiration and challenge. In particular, one story has stayed with me, in which newly freed Black women and men are searching along the long dusty roads of the USA for lost relatives torn away from each other by the institutionalised brutality of slavery. I hoped I might acknowledge the power of that title, *Long Journey Home*, and apply it to this anthology, because it seems to me that, as lesbians, we have been separated from one another for so long, worldwide, often trapped within what Adrienne Rich has called the institutions of compulsory heterosexuality.

The lesbian writers in this book take their courage into their hands to tell it how it is – how we are still losing and finding each other. These stories are sometimes funny and glad, other times disturbing and poignant. Across time and place, class, nationality and ethnicity these writers ask: Where is home? Is it inside us? Is it with a partner? Is it a place? A country? All or none of these?

How do we find the strength to move on, from situations, places, or relationships that are not good for us, when the straight world around us doesn't know or care? As more than one of the stories here shows us, there are still women torn apart from themselves and/or their partners in denial, doubt and sorrow. We know that the reasons are cultural and historical, personal and political.

Nevertheless we do, sometimes, find one another. We find creativity and joy, sensuality and eroticism, laughter and fun, friendship and new families. Some stories here show long-term relationships where, against a backdrop of commitment and support, significant actions, decisions and journeys are undertaken: journeys to the centre of the self, journeys alone or with others; journeys through other lands.

We are real, and we always have been, as the historical contributions dare to tell us. We publish them here because all lesbians have a right to lesbian cultural continuity. The myth that lesbianism is a western thing, or that it is a recent thing, is one of the powerful tools that may be wielded to cleave us apart.

Long Journey Home, as a title, sits in intriguing contradiction to the newness of the writers, thus providing a marvellous opportunity for creative exploration. The writing by these contributors starts in a context quite separate from my work, when I was a new lesbian writer twenty years ago. And while some of the themes are universal, many too are different. Herein lies the interest for me as editor – new voices, new challenges, new demands for our rights. I have no illusions about how hard it can be for a woman to come out as a lesbian. Until every lesbian is as free as every heterosexual woman to show her feelings in public – holding hands, arms around her friends, just being herself – our everyday rights as lesbians will continue to be claimed. Until every young girl has a safe, fulfilling childhood, in which she also knows of lesbianism as a real and optimistic possibility for her, which, if she chose it, would bring joy to her parents or guardians, there will be renewed demands for lesbian equality.

It is twenty-one years since I left my two young children (then ages nine and seven) with their father, in order to live openly as a lesbian, and we all began the long and magnificent process of mending. I wake each morning as a published writer having found my own voice, self-assurance and certainty in my lesbian body. In my bone marrow, the word dyke runs through like Brighton rock. My sons are grown men, warm, generous human beings who say, 'Go for it, Mum. You made the choice to leave your marriage (and us) to be true to your self, and because of you we know we're free to make our own decisions, to lead our own lives, in the ways that seem best for us. We love you, Mum. Because of you we know about life after separation and happiness again after loss.' I have a wonderful life-partner, Cynth Morris, my trusted friend for over eleven years before we re-met, laughing with recognition, and fell in love.

Meanwhile, the recent transformations in my personal life have run parallel to the exciting work of searching for the contributors to this anthology. I would like to thank Charlotte Cole, at The Women's Press, for her skilful support, tact and tenacity as we guided this project towards its completion. I am thrilled to be the editor of this book, which has brought me into contact with so many new lesbian writers. For me this collection has brought a life-affirming sense of community involving national and international communication, and a stimulating exchange of ideas within a warm context of new lesbian friendships. It has been a wonderful Long Journey Home.

Caeia March
From a Devon hillside

Storm

Samantha Bakhurst

'We talked a lot about life. There was nothing else to talk about.'

Amanda Vail (1921–1966)

There was going to be a storm. Sometimes you just know it. On today, of all days. And now Cammy's tongue recoiled as the taste of metal travelled along it. She screwed her eyes up until they were further than shut. Not that. The taste of ammonia. Like Jif, like hospital corridors, gagging, in the throat and now, here, inside her head. The small, two-bedroomed flat was quiet and empty and Cammy gasped. Silently, inwardly, knowing what was to come next. Why did this always happen when she was alone? Not that it would make any difference if Jake or her mum were there. It would feel just as empty – inside and out. Apart from the impending storm and now, of course, this. She just wished it were not today. Of all days. Cammy loosened her grip on the magazine she had been looking at and dropped it to one side. The smooth glossiness of white smiles lay crushed and damp next to her single bed. She leaped up and pulled a sweatshirt out of the dirty linen bag in the corner. Nothing else clean, Mum and Jake out, but Cammy didn't care. She had decided not to care. The stretched neck of the grey sweatshirt squashed down her hair and made it shiver and stand on end in single strands. Cammy grinned angrily at the girl in the mirror. That thirteen-year-old with hair standing to attention, her stained top hanging loose, whose right eye was beginning to twitch, tick tick, an enemy twitch today, for God's sake.

Through the metal cased windows, third floor up on Vivaldi Estate, the sky blew past. Dark, growling, threatening, it rolled by and the thirteen-year-old pressed her cheek up against the cold glass. The dizziness was starting. Cammy knew the routine so well, yet it always terrified her. The cold window soothed the throbbing but the storm sat heavy just above and wasn't helping matters. It was funny that. How we can feel it when there's going to be a storm. Like dogs or something. Like knowing you were going to have an attack, an episode. A raindrop thudded against her left ear.

'Are you sodding aiming at me or something?' she shouted, at no one in particular, but eyes skywards. And, in response, the patter of drops chasing close behind. Like the sound of that funny orchestra Mrs Frome, the old lady downstairs, always played on a Sunday night. Starting off quiet, like an old man sleeping at the back of a bus. Then growing, making your toes curl, not knowing why. Then your mum's shouting: 'Keep the frigging noise down you deaf old bat!' And the lady turns it down so that your mum can listen to the telly louder. Rhythmic rain. Like in a nursery rhyme. Patter patter, rat-tat, whoosh. Cammy stepped backwards, unsure as to whether she should go or not. Well, to be honest she *knew* she definitely shouldn't go, but who'd find out? And more to the point, who'd care? And it was today, after all. Sod it.

Before she could change her mind, before she was feeling too dizzy and lost to the world, she put the front door on the latch (possibly a mistake since Robert, the druggie on the first floor, was back on the estate) and ran out into the cold rain and blustering waves of wind. Cammy loved thunder and lightning. It scared her, but it was so big and exciting it was irresistible. And she hated having an attack which made her feel small, alone and sucked away. The two together might make her feel better somehow. She pounded along the walkway, rusted metal thudding with

2

each footfall. She was going up to the top to watch it all. London below, falling away like an imperial township. Then the sky, and of course the wonderful display. The fireworks of the earth.

You see, there is a small door which should be locked. It is on the left of the lifts as you reach the top floor. Only two people in the whole building know that the door is, in fact, unlocked. Cammy is person number one.

The lift jolted to a halt. Already there were sparks behind the clouds. As if a light bulb were swinging on a chain behind the cloudy walls. Raindrops fell free in the wind and the storm breathed louder and louder. Cammy stumbled out of the lift. This was a bad attack, she could hardly stand up. The physicality of the weather held her to the outside world where normally she drifted away. She dragged herself over to the door and reached the lock. It had not been touched. She was still the only storm chaser on the estate.

Cammy shivered and her pinched red fingers manoeuvred the lock. Some people were better than others at opening doors. Twist the bolt, under its rusted cage, until it slides, a release like a sigh as you lean back into a hot bath, and the lock is unlocked, freed, open. Cammy's fingers were lithe and adept, unlike her mother's, especially when they shook, which was nearly always. The view from the top of Vivaldi's Estate was like a New York film set. Buildings stretched nose to sky, and the natural squares from Islington, Camden and beyond carved shapes into the lines of traffic and wintry trees. Cammy knelt against the railings, all rusted and decaying. The world was moving away from her now as it always did when she had one of those episode things. Doctor Vrahimedes had talked over Cammy's head at her mother.

'The MRI scan was clear. Apart from more invasive explorations, I can't offer much apart from to say everything seems quite all right. Perhaps it's a hormonal thing. I mean, at thirteen, the body undergoes a lot of changes.'

'What're you saying? Is there or isn't there something wrong with her?' Her mum was beginning to fidget. She liked clear answers that were black and white. Like at school reports evening, twisting around on the plastic chair, knee bouncing up and down: 'Yeah, yeah, made some improvements, but do I ground her or take her to McDonald's?' Now, sitting before the irritated doctor, her mum clutched the shopping bag which sat on her lap and demanded a clear answer. 'Is she ill or not?'

He tried to be patient. He tried to spell it out for her. 'We don't know. But at the moment we can't find anything so we think it might be a virus of some kind. These…episodes she's been having. Well, this happens sometimes with girls her age.' Episodes. Good word. Like an episode of *EastEnders*. Or some section of a poem like 'City. A treatise in four episodes.' So Cammy had episodes. Yet one more thing to make her feel different. Great.

Once you were past the door, the roof of the estate was strange. Not how you'd expect it to look at all. There was a long flat section of roof, slate coloured. Then there was this groove along the centre, which looked as if it were designed to collect rain. Which was exactly what it did do. Then, at one end of the roof there was a small enclosure. Someone could definitely set up home and live here. The enclosure had two walls, a roof of its own, two benches and a little wooden locker. Which was locked. Cammy lay back on the dry bench and looked through her dizziness at the black clouds that felt so close you could almost stick your head through their outer layer and shout 'Coooeee' to God. She'd like to have a conversation with God. Despite everything, she had to smile. There she was, like a pinched chicken at the bottom of the deep freeze, pink skin popping up all over with the cold, head spinning uncontrollably because of the old hormones, no one to talk to about…well, about anything actually. But she had her secret terrace. Her own London hideaway.

Suddenly, Cammy was seized by a quiet, minute but disturbing observation. The railings that divided the hideaway from the rest of the roof were broken on one side. A small break, unnoticeable to the unfamiliar eye. But Cammy knew. Someone had been there. Someone might be there now.

Quickly, Cammy staggered to her feet and scanned the roof. Only rain, swirling, freezing rain and her. The episode was biting at her tongue, making her cheek burn, as if it were dissolving. For each time it burned, some fragment of sensation was lost in the skin.

'Don't move little lady. I got you in my sights. Don't move.' Cammy did as she was told and stood, or rather swayed, like she was holding the ball in netball. The voice drowned in the sounds of wind, rain and fear. A second person, another storm chaser, the other key holder to the secret place on top of the world.

Normally her episode would have subsided by now but fear made it worse. Cammy wanted to cry but this was something she hadn't done since she was six and a half. The voice bubbled to the surface.

'What is it? Hey, what's wrong?' Cammy turned round. Eli stood staring, chewing his gum slower than she'd ever seen him chew. Cammy felt like throwing her arms around his neck. 'Only kidding. Yeah? I thought you was gonna cry for a second. What you doing up here? You're from the third floor, ain't yer? What's your name again?'

'Cammy.' She paused. 'How do you know about this place?'

Eli's jaw worked faster as he thrust his hands into his pockets and his shoulders relaxed, as though they began to dance to some silent music. 'How come you do?'

'I found it last year. I didn't think anyone else knew about it.'

'Yeah? Well, I do.' Eli frowned, then he sat on the unbroken railings on the other side of the enclosure. Cammy realised that her episode had passed. She watched Eli, then sat back on the bench again, hands on her knees like her mum had told her to in front of boys. Not that she ever wore a skirt or anything but she thought maybe it was a special signal like a green light or GO sign so she closed her knees. Eli was tall and slim. He must have been nearly fifteen. She had seen him with his friends down by the bins. The other boys had been hitting the sides of the metal containers with sticks and making a din, forcing Danny Partridge, the guy from the corner flat, to come out and yell at them. They never took any notice, though. Kept right on banging. Ended up setting fire to one of them. Eli didn't seem so lawless up here under the sky.

'I sometimes get these things called episodes. They're inside my head. Not like I'm a lunatic or a schizophrenic or anything. I get this weird feeling. It's an illness...' Cammy had never said these things out loud before. It was like a rehearsal. 'I...I can't explain but it hurts and it helps to get outside. So I come up here. I didn't know anyone else knew about the place.'

'Yeah – you said.' Eli's attention was split between the receding storm and some Rizla papers he was extracting from a leg pocket in his combats. Out came a silken paper, then a second, allowing a third, spare piece to offer itself up for a subsequent occasion, like a tongue or a finger beckoning, tempting. Then he put the Rizlas back into his leg pocket while the remaining two papers fought against the dying wind. Quicker than Cammy could blow her nose, Eli had licked, squared, torn the two papers and secured them as one much longer one. Sweetly, teased out using the tip of a tongue, his long brown fingers caressed the paper, smoothing down the joins, like an artist. His eyes moved between the storm taking its leave, and the job in hand. Never at Cammy, not once. Then he set about laying down the bed of tobacco, burning some black and crumbling the melted, sweet-smelling crumbs along the length of the paper. He eased it all into place and then his tongue was back on duty, pulling the sides together, creating the perfect tube of pleasure.

'I keep a pet here an' all. What do you reckon to that?' Eli swung round, a twinkle in his eye.

'What do you mean?'

'I'll show you, if you ask me nicely.'

'Oh.' Cammy had a brother and didn't like this kind of game. There was always one more pretty please or I swear I'll wash your dishes for a month, no matter how nicely she asked. Sod that.

Eli laughed. 'Come here.'

He hopped off the railings and took a key out of his pocket. At the side of the enclosure there was a ledge without a barrier. It was about six inches wide and overlooked the road, which was a long way down. Eli started along the ledge as though it were a pavement. He glanced over his shoulder. 'Come on. Just don't look down.'

Cammy watched Eli striding along, then her eyes gazed at the steep drop. 'I can't.'

Eli clicked his tongue and waved his arms. 'Trust me, it's a cinch. Don't think about it.'

Cammy was good at not thinking about things. Her mum had taught her not to ask stupid questions that had no answers, like 'Why doesn't Dad come over any more?' or 'Where are you when you don't come home, Mum?' She had learned not to think about the things that she knew Jake got up to on his way to and from school. And she refused to think about how she felt about things. Anything. So then there's this guy standing in front of you, holding out his hand and saying walk, just don't think. And he has a mystery key and a mystery pet. Cammy screwed her eyes tight, opened them with courage and determination and she took a step forward. That wasn't too bad. So she took another and then another. Eli's hand was only a couple of steps away. She concentrated on his hand, trust me, those long fingers.

The loose slate fell, tripping over the drainpipe like a clumsy ballerina. Then it swirled round and down, tugged by the wind, this way and that, lost in the camouflage of the trees opposite before smashing onto the pavement on the other side of the street. Cammy's left leg had begun the descent with the slate, her right tangled awkwardly behind in the drainpipe. And Eli leaned over, his long fingers stiff and taut, stretching the grey sweatshirt beyond recognition. Their eyes followed the slate. As it smashed below, Cammy looked back at Eli, her eyes wide, not with the fear of having nearly fallen to her death, but surprised at Eli's agility and her own lack of interest in what may have become of her.

'It's my birthday today.' Cammy whispered, her voice caught in the neck of the sweatshirt. Eli rolled his eyes and exhaled a long, slow breath. Then he pulled her back, Cammy scrambling against the wall, just like trying to get out of the swimming pool, until they sat, crumpled, together on the ledge.

'You're going back inside.'

'But I want to see your pet. You told me I could see your pet.'

'You can see it another day. You're going back.'

'I'm not going until I see your pet.' Cammy's folded arms disguised her returning anxiety, five storeys up above London cement. Her eyes darted down briefly before looking back at Eli defiantly. He examined Cammy's face for the first time, the twinkle returning to his eye, then he leaned back against the uneven wall behind and took a few more long, slow breaths.

'Why aren't you at school today, anyway?'

'Who are you? My bloody father? Why aren't you?' Cammy gripped her sleeves from beneath her folded arms.

'Yeah, right. Because I'm bunking, that's why.'

'Oh.' That was pretty straightforward.

'And now you're going back.' Eli was adamant. Cammy was a little relieved. 'Shuffle your arse along backwards. I'm not doing that shit again. Besides you nearly wrecked my smoke.' He held out the twisted tube of white as an illustration. It looked like a used pipe cleaner. Cammy shuffled. If there was one thing Jake had taught her, it was never to get between a man and his smoke.

Once back at the enclosure, Eli smoothed out his joint and put it between his lips. Gently, lovingly, like it could save the world. Then he pulled out a silver lighter that flipped open and sparked up in one unbroken gesture. The flame lit his face in the darkening afternoon. He frowned, concentrating, single-minded, slow. And as he inhaled and closed his eyes, Cammy looked around her. She couldn't believe that it was still just her and Eli out here.

'You smoke?' Eli's sleepy eyes questioned Cammy. She looked down and shook her head. Jake was right. She was just a dumb girl – scared of heights, dizzy, lame and now uncool. 'What you doing for your birthday then?'

'Nothing much.'

'You got a boyfriend?'

Cammy shook her head. 'What's your pet?'

'Na-ah, I'm not tellin' ya – you'll have to wait.'

'But I may die, I might get run over and then I'll never know...'

'You ain't gonna die. And anyway, even if you do, it won't matter because you won't know nothin' anyway.'

'How do you know I'm not gonna die, stupid?'

'I just know.'

Cammy pulled a strand of hair behind her ear. She half-closed her eyes and looked up at Eli lazily. Then she leaned forward and whispered, 'But it's my birthday.' He recoiled.

'Don't flirt with me! You don't need to do that stuff up here. Let's make it our rule. Up here, you can be who you want. Okay. You can say what you want...'

They sat in silence, while Eli pulled on the last moments of his smoke, burning his lips and screwing up his face. Then he threw the butt over the edge and lay back on the bench. Cammy was trying hard to think about what she wanted to be.

'I think I'd like to be a man.'

Eli opened his eyes and twisted round to look at Cammy, as if that would explain what she had just said.

'I'd like to be a man so as I could do lots of things.'

'Like what?'

'Like be a singer in a band or be a spy...'

'You could be a singer...'

'Or hang out after dark and look at 'peds...'

'Ahh, 'peds...'

'Or kiss a woman...'

Eli twisted right round. 'You wanna kiss a woman?' His high-pitched voice suddenly sounded very loud. Cammy looked down.

'Just to know what it's like. You know?' He looked at her for what seemed like hours. Then he relaxed and slouched back against the bench.

'Yeah, man, I know what you mean. Not that I haven't kissed a woman, ya kna...'

'Innit?' Cammy smiled. She was allowed to think about kissing a woman. She had been given permission to dream. She had spoken the words out loud, tested them out up here under the clouds and nothing bad had happened. Maybe God wasn't punishing her. Maybe love could wash in on any wave. Give me a roof to tell secrets on and I will find my birthday gift. The one I gave myself. Suddenly Cammy was filled with an incredible energy. She was ready to sit up, leap up, open her arms and legs and spring into the clouds, pull faces, eat chocolate, dance to the jazz music played quietly behind the walls of her bedroom, that made her shiver and laugh into her pillow. And put her lips up against Maja Raban, the shy refugee who sat at the back of the class, who had once held her hand down by the lake.

'Man, it's getting late an' I'm starving. I'm gonna head down. You wanna come?'

Cammy shook her head, trying to look serious but with a smile that was threatening to take over her face. Eli touched her shoulder as he bounced along gently, sucking his teeth as a form of habit. 'See you up here again.' It was almost a question. Almost, but not quite. As he reached the door, he turned round. 'Happy birthday, yeah. I'll show you the pigeon next time.'

'A pigeon? I nearly killed myself to look at your pigeon?'

Eli laughed and slunk out of the door. Cammy wandered over to the edge of the roof and looked at her picture of London. The lights of the high-rise blocks were uniform and comforting against the dark belt of the disappearing storm. You could make out the orange glow of the lift as it shifted people up and down, discharging them with precision at the requested floor. Below, the boys were gathering round at the beginning of the night. She recognised Sol and Fernando. They claimed the streets and clamoured to be heard. Then she saw Eli saunter over, crisps in hand, and sit on the seat of a parked moped, joining in with their stupid banter.

She smiled and backed away, heading for the door. It was her birthday and Cammy's turn to claim what was hers. A single piece of crumpled paper, ripped from her Homework Diary. The one she had opened twenty times, at least. The one which had Maja's phone number on, written hastily. And the word 'Yeah' with an exclamation mark.

Coming Home
Cea Vulliamy

I took her down to the water on the first night there to show
her the phosphorescence. She was delighted by the faint
green glow, and before I knew it, she had her shirt off and
was standing there bare-breasted in the moonlight, waist-
deep in the tumbling waves. I sat on the rocks that framed
the beach, feeling clumsy but happy. The beach stretched
out wide; fine, but dirty sand and little rolling waves. Above
the beach, the sea front was lined with cheap cafés and
tacky arcades. They'd pulled down the holiday camp where
my parents stayed before they moved here. I had avoided
everything to do with South Wales for the seven years since
I left; I'd forgotten how it felt to be 'home'.

She was waving and calling for me to join her and I
wanted to, but was embarrassed by her nakedness. How
long was it since I had seen another human body unclothed?
I had never been able to imagine myself naked, even half-
naked, in front of somebody else, and felt almost puzzled at
her ability to stand there waving at me with all that taut
skin visible. She flipped and disappeared into a wave and
suddenly I missed her. What an admission! My heart
thumped louder for a moment, but I reminded myself that
no one had heard the thought. There had been more and
more of them, these dangerous thoughts.

In the car on the way down to Barry from the cold grey
of Newcastle she had slept, a gentle snoring with the rise

and fall of her chest. At some point I had noticed her hand resting on her thigh. It was a small hand, with beautiful thin fingers, the veins on the back of it raised slightly, which I had always thought attractive. My own hands were fleshy and square, the skin on my palms, at the base of my fingers was flaky and eczematous. I was still faintly disgusted at myself for wearing the lovely jade ring on such an unlovely finger. And there it was, I was imagining those fingers of hers interlocked with mine – the audacity of the thought! I'd always known I was a lesbian, but desire had always felt too frightening a concept for me to act upon it. I pushed the thought swiftly from me, pretended it wasn't mine, but the image wouldn't leave me.

She appeared again, wet hair plastered to her skull. I looked away quickly as she turned towards me.

'Come on!' she called, 'Come on, it's really lovely.' She was laughing and smiling. 'It's such a lovely night, you can't honestly tell me that you want to sit there with all your clothes on all night?'

No, I thought, *I can't honestly tell you that I want to, but I can honestly say that I think I have to.*

When we arrived at the house that afternoon, she let out a little squeal and dropped her bags to dance up and down the steps up to the tired blue door.

'Oh, it's lovely!' and she flung her arms around me, her body pressed tightly to mine as I stood there rigidly, foolishly. I don't know if she felt it, but she let go of me quickly and I was at once thankful and sorry.

'Come on, where's the key? Quickly, I want to see if it's as lovely inside as it is out!'

I fumbled in my bag for the key and let us inside. She scampered off ahead of me and I could hear her exclaiming excitedly at each small room as she came to it. I picked up her bags from where she had dropped them and carried them to the first of the two bedrooms. It had been my room for those long years when I had lived here with my family. Somebody had replaced the little metal-framed bed with an expensive-looking wooden double one, but it was still the lovely cobalt blue I had chosen the summer I was fifteen. A new coat, but the same shade. White sheets stretched across the bed and the quilt my father's mother had made was folded neatly at the foot of it. I shuddered at the thought of him, pushed his memory quickly away. Christ still hung stiffly from the wooden cross above the bed. I used to wonder if He really was all-seeing, whether He watched us every night from the wall, making mental notes to tell Saint Peter what an evil little girl I was and not, on any account, to let me into Heaven come Judgement Day.

'Bollocks,' I whispered as loud as I dared and, shuddering again, left the room.

She was standing in front of me now, saying something to me.

'What? Sorry, I was miles away.'

'I said, you're going to have to come in now, look!'

I looked round and saw that the tide had swept around my perch and I would indeed have to get into the water unless I clambered back to the sand barefoot over sharp rock. She was swimming away again. I stood up wondering whether this meant that I had to take my clothes off too, but decided that they would get wet anyway, so I slid down off the rock.

I had decided that it would be safer to put her in my old room and for me to sleep in what had been my parents' room; the last thing I wanted, for her or for me, was night terrors, and I was sure they would come if I slept in my room. It hadn't really occurred to me until I walked into the crisp brightness of my parents' room that this was all mine. There had always been photographs of them and me in the room. Now I could turn the photographs away, throw out my mother's hideous ornaments – everything that had made the room belong to somebody could be discarded or destroyed. I was an only child, so there was no fuss, everything came straight to me. There was a small amount of money that Dad hadn't had time to drink before he died, and this place with a relatively small amount of mortgage left to pay. I understood from Mrs Williams next door that he hadn't been out much since my mother died, and had talked about trying to sell it and go back up the Valleys, which had always remained home to him. There were plenty of others like him on the estate who had jumped at the right to buy in the eighties when Thatcher promised a ticket into the elusive world of the 'upwardly mobile', and now they were stuck with poorly built or too small homes, or just wishes for something a bit better, but they knew they would never be able to sell. But standing there in that room, ready to be emptied of memories, ready for me to create my own, new ones, I was happy, so happy that the one thing that could make a difference to me had been saved. It was terrifying being here, but for the first time since I was sixteen and running fiercely away from them, sinking into the sea of faces at Cardiff Central, for the first time since then, I felt like I had a huge and joyous opportunity.

The water was cold. My baggy T-shirt clung to me in places and flapped about me in others. I wanted to enjoy this, and in a fit of carelessness, I hauled it off me and threw it to the shore, turning, horrified as it left my hand and I heard her clapping and cheering from a couple of metres off. Too late now, so I threw myself under the water and swam hard, out and along, parallel to the beach. I could feel the water moving beneath my belly and breasts. Oh God, my belly, I had to be able to hide it from her. I swam harder and calmed myself, *It's night, there really isn't enough light for her to see you that well*. I swam on, but the feeling of unguarded ease I'd had when I took my shirt off had escaped me and after a few moments I turned and swam back towards her.

'See, I told you it was wonderful didn't I?'

She was treading water, beaming at me.

'Yeah, yeah, it is wonderful,' I said. 'But I think I'm going to get out now. I want to finish that bottle of wine and then I want black coffee on the back step, and then bed.'

'Sounds good to me. Oh, unless you want some time alone.'

'No. No, I want you to come and share it with me.'

Could too much be read into that?

'I'll be drunk if you leave me to the wine on my own!'

I hoped the addition didn't sound too hasty, too much like a quick escape, but she didn't seem to notice, she was already swimming for the shore and our clothes. I panicked, *She mustn't get there before me, I must have time to put my shirt back on before she gets there.* But there was no way that I could beat her back. I hunched over as I came out of the water. The tide had come in further and was beginning to lap at my shirt so at least I didn't have to be exposed for long before I reached it. I know she saw them, the great purple scars across my belly and upper thighs, even in the dull moonlight.

They were too big and too dark. But she didn't say anything, nor did she allow her eyes to dwell on them. I was grateful. We walked back up to the house in silence. I was afraid.

In the living room, half a bottle of wine later and on my way to fetch another one, I shocked myself by turning in the kitchen doorway and saying aloud, 'God, d'you know, this is all mine?'

She looked at me hesitantly and nodded.

'This place and two thousand pounds.' I paused, taking the thought in. 'It feels amazing.'

'Are you okay? Are you sad?'

'No, I'm not. I'm quite scared, but I'm actually happy.'

'What do you want to do now?'

'I don't really know. I think I want to give up everything and move back here 'cause it feels good to be here. It feels like an opportunity and it feels like I'm owed it in some way,' I grinned, 'but I don't know. I suppose it's quite a lot to take in really.'

'I'll bet.'

'What would you do?'

'I'd leave everything back home, give up work and live here. Spend the rest of my days lazing on the beach, playing the arcades, eating fresh fish and chips, none of that crap you get in Newcastle, and not doing anything remotely taxing. There. What d'you reckon?'

'Sounds blissful.'

We sank into an easy silence, each of us dreaming something better for ourselves.

Later, on the step with coffee, she asked if she could hold my hand. I thought about feeling guilty for imagining it in the car. I flinched, but couldn't say no. The shock of touch was sharp, though not painful as I had expected it to be. Nobody had touched me like that for a long, long time and despite myself, I found myself aching to be held, to be rocked like a baby. I was staring down at the lights from the arcades on the island, willing the feeling to go away, and quickly. I could feel my tear ducts burning and was determined not to suffer the indignity of crying. I breathed deeply. It was very late and we were both drunk on wine and happiness, the muggy evening and the smell of honeysuckle that managed to creep out from under the weeds in the overgrown garden; no wonder I was feeling strange. The tears were filling my eyes and soon would be trembling on the lower lids and spilling down my face. I began a steady chant somewhere in the back of my head, *it is dark, it is dark, it is dark.*

'Where did they come from?'

I spun round to face her. I could feel my eyes wide with surprise and tears scooting sideways as I turned.

'What?' I screamed inwardly at the unmasked terror in my voice.

'Those scars.'

How could she ask so matter-of-factly? Why couldn't she be afraid of them, of me, like everybody else? Had she no idea of what she was asking me? And then the great pit of shame was there, gaping and ugly beneath my feet, I was sinking into the ooze and slime and wishing for all my life that the world really would swallow me up. I opened and shut my mouth several times, but there was no air in my lungs to push out past my vocal chords, and what could I say anyway? And then out of nowhere I had an image of myself sitting there with my mouth opening and closing and I thought I must look like a drowning fish and I laughed uncontrollably.

'I'm sorry,' I gasped eventually, 'I'm sorry. I just thought for a minute...' I felt too foolish to explain my laughter, but I had to explain something, 'I did them myself.'

She didn't hear me, and leaned closer, still holding my hand.

'I'm sorry, I didn't hear you. What did you say?'

I felt I was choking on all that shame, I was making strange gurgling noises where my breath was stuck in my throat. I closed my eyes and focused on my heartbeat.

'I did them myself.' I whispered again and couldn't open my eyes. Her fingers gripped my hand tighter and more tears came squeezing out of me in response. I breathed deep into a long quiet.

'D'you want to go to bed? D'you want me to stay up with you? What is the best thing I can do now to help?'

With my eyes still sealed shut with my crying, I opened my arms to her, reaching up and around her and she held on to me tightly for a long time. My insides shook violently, *She wants to help, she wants to help me, she saw that I'm hurt and she wants to help me.* It was a mixture of pure fear and pure elation and for once I could cope with it, with her arms warm around me, it felt so good.

She helped me inside and to my bed; my body was still shaking too much to manage it alone. She asked me if I wanted help to get undressed and I nodded and again her eyes did not dwell on the ugly marks. She pulled the sheet over me.

'Call me if you want me.'

She turned the light out as she left the room and I waited in the dark until I heard her climb into her own bed before I climbed shakily out of mine to turn it back on.

I woke sweating and breathing hard. The sweat pooled in the small of my back and the sheet was sticking to my skin. *He's gone*, I told myself, *you're safe now, he's dead and gone.* But the shadows appeared under my door before I had fully settled myself in reality and I slipped into panic. My head spun and a nausea rose in the pit of my stomach. Somewhere outside of myself, as if from a great distance, I heard a whimper, and I was no longer in my body, but looking down at it. And it wasn't mine and the panic rose. I was looking at, not my own twenty-three-year-old body, but my thirteen-year-old self and the shadows were still under the door and I could hear his breathing. I counted the seconds until he opened the door. It wasn't Dad. I felt back into my body and found myself sobbing. She put the tray she was carrying down in the doorway and came to the bedside.

'What's happened?'

She offered me her arms, but I couldn't stand the thought of being touched, however much I wanted to be. She opened the curtains, letting the light stream into the room and waited anxiously.

'I made tea, do you want some?'

I nodded.

'Hold on then, I think I've got some Rescue Remedy somewhere.'

She returned a few moments later and dropped the remedy into a glass of water. My hands were shaking and I kept spilling it, but she stayed by me, her hands over mine on the glass, and I accepted the touch.

'You want to talk now?' she asked, when my shaking and crying had finally subdued.

'Let me get dressed.'

We walked up to the town and down again, past the big posh houses with their steeply sloping front gardens and big front doors. The road sloped hard down towards the park and the beach. This beach was smaller and quieter than the island, no sand unless the tide was right out, just grey stones. It was bleak and quite strange in its uniform greyness, but was definitely my favourite of Barry's two beaches. This had been the place I escaped to, a place to still the panic in me that, in those terror-filled days, had been almost constant. Down here I would sit for long hours, careless of the letters the school sent home. Mother was already ill by then. I never did see her again after I ran from them at the station. I like to think that perhaps she understood and didn't hurt that her only daughter wasn't there for her in those last few months.

It was down here that I had met Huw the summer before I ran away. He was younger than me, but always seemed infinitely wiser. We never used to talk much, he just showed me things, creatures, fossils and shells, fish heads he'd found, discarded by the boys whose fathers had the time and inclination to take them fishing. We used to swim together too, out as far as we dared, punching hard against the tide, there was desperation in every stroke, with every kick we were kicking out our pain. We both knew something terrible was happening for both of us. I often saw bruises and huge welts on his body; I don't know how much he saw of my terror, but he knew it was there, though we never spoke about it. He was here on holiday with his family for a long month, but it wasn't until a few days before he left to go back home that I told him my plan to run away. His dark eyes glazed and for a brief moment I saw just how much younger than me he was; probably only nine or ten. He touched his forefinger to my collar bone; I think the touch was meant for my heart, but he was afraid of touching my small breasts. He said, quietly, 'Run fast.' That was the last time anybody touched me so gently, so purposefully.

It was so peaceful down there on the beach. The early morning sun was bright and sending little sparks of light off the waves. Over on the east side of the beach where the water was deep beneath the rocks Huw used to play amongst, the spray spouted up and came cascading down in tiny rainbow droplets, like fairy lights. I think it was that moment – watching the sun on the sea spray, feeling it warming me through my cotton shirt, being easily aware of the woman at my side – I decided that nobody, living or dead was going to take this from me. This was owed me. It was indeed a tremendous possibility. There I was at twenty-three years old, and suddenly I didn't need to struggle any more. The mortgage repayments were less than half the rent I was paying on the poky little council flat in Newcastle, and I knew I could find enough work down here to manage, and there was no longer the possibility of Dad finding me. I had this beautiful place; my life was truly beginning.

'I'm okay now.' I smiled, and she smiled back, full of sun.

'I'm glad.'

'Thanks for coming with me.'

'Hey, thank you, I'm touched that you should want me to come with you. And God knows, I was so sick of the office, and I would never have been able to get away like this without you.'

'So it's good for both of us then?'

She hugged me for an answer, and I hugged her back, tentatively, and not without a little fear, but I hugged her.

*

'Oh, it feels weird sometimes, you know?' I was talking quietly over the table in the café-cum-newsagents. 'Like at the office; everybody being so sweet and concerned 'cause my father's dead, and I'm just not sure what to do with it.'

'How d'you mean?'

'I don't know how to say it without giving the wrong impression of myself.' I pushed a piece of lettuce around my plate trying to figure out how to say enough without saying too much. 'My dad was a bit of a bastard.' The lettuce moved round again. 'Actually he was a fucking great bastard. And I don't much care that he's dead. Only in so far as I never told him what I thought of him. I wish I'd had the courage, the rage to do that before he died.'

She was nodding at me. She didn't say anything, didn't look angry.

'Do you think I'm an awful person for thinking all that?'

'No, of course I don't. I think you're a very lovely person and I'm really glad, honoured, that you feel able to talk to me. It feels like a gift.'

That minute, just for a small, dangerous minute, I wanted to reach across the table and kiss her. I slammed the thought away as fast as I could, but it left a slightly sweet taste in my mouth. She was saying something to me.

'Could you handle it if I asked you a very forward and maybe intrusive question?'

I swallowed again on my wicked thought and nodded.

'Did your dad abuse you?'

I saw stars. I was reeling and trying to get up and knocking chairs over and a glass spun from the table in slow motion.

'I think I'm going to be sick.'

I don't remember anything else.

She told me I wasn't out for long. I woke up to her and the boy from behind the counter flapping the dishcloth over me. They gave me a glass of water and the poor boy was terrified thinking his food was responsible. I sat up slowly, expecting a head rush, but I was fine, and spent the next fifteen minutes trying to persuade them to believe me. The young man refused payment for our meal and we straggled home, her full of apologies and trying to help me walk. The only reason I was having trouble walking was because I was laughing so much at the image of me keeling over sideways and pulling half the contents of the table with me. I was still giggling back at the house as I tried to wash the worst of the salad dressing out of my shirt. She was pacing up and down behind me in the kitchen.

'I really am so sorry, I can't believe I was so insensitive to you. To you of all people! I'm horrified at myself.'

'Shut up!' I laughed, and she stopped, mid-stride, mouth still open.

'Nobody ever bothered to ask me that before. It wasn't insensitive, it was absolutely what I needed to hear.'

I turned back to the sink and my shirt, watching my hands move in the water. 'Anyway, the answer's yes. My dad did abuse me all the time we lived here.'

'I'm sorry,' she said slowly, resting a hand on my shoulder.

I took her hand and turned to face her. 'So am I.'

And with my mouth full of fear and a slight tremble that straddled the border between that fear and a welling excitement, I kissed her.

The Recognition Scene
Frances Bingham

There is the usual bustle front-of-house. In the bars, cloakrooms, foyers, ladies', gents', the auditorium and the many stairways, people are getting ready for their evening. Outside, where the main entrance, lighted, illuminates the whole street, more people are arriving, stepping up slow to the bright portico as though they cross onto the stage itself when they pass through those wide, brass-detailed doors. Within, it glitters; the interior glows through bevelled glass engraved and curlicued. The shallow, sweeping stairs are red-carpeted, gold-rodded; mirrors in huge gilt frames reflect them endlessly, and multiply the many people passing into myriads. A massive chandelier sparkles above the foyer, its electrical magnificence is specially advertised. We Londoners are not dazzled; not by this nor by the stucco nymphs whose charms are so invitingly displayed in niches decorating the stairway. We have seen it all before. Golden draperies, tastefully placed on smiling women, even the cherubs voluptuous and knowing; we expect no less.

This haphazard half-mile of lit-up buildings is the centre of our Empire, which is to say the world. They say that if you wait in Leicester Square – or is it Piccadilly? – for long enough, everyone you have ever known will pass you by. (That *would* be inconvenient.) Tonight, not even Saturday, and the hall will be full to its capacity, the biggest in the world – except America – and crammed from stalls to ceiling in inverse hierarchy, the richest at the bottom. Already the street is at a standstill, the pavement blocked with audience arriving. Each column has its little skirt of loungers, each pilaster and corner shelters women.

Up the first flight of stairs, beyond the gilded, oak-railed banisters and through a vigorous grove of potted palms, is my place, at one end of the long bar. I can see the women float smoothly up to the entrance, posture perfect. The manager in his brocade waistcoat is bowing, calculating the ladies' worth in jewellery while keeping his little red eyes away from their bosoms. The poor folk who arrive and clatter up to the gallery from the side entrances bring in the cold on their jackets, a whiff of outdoors. But here the perfume is hothouse; roses in buttonholes, scented bodies and sherry-tinted breath. The men are in black and white, of course, like magpies, burnished with starch and brilliantine, crispness and shine. The women are wearing shades of purple this season, beaded drapes in crushed velvet, devoré, Fortuny pleat silks in grape, violet, wine, plum; richness and harvest ripe for the magpies' picking.

I know them all, these eager, excitable people. There are the inky clerks who have to hurry from work; the youths in their flamboyant, crumpled suits, denying frayed trouser hems and worn-away heels with over-loud laughter, and the working women, sober-coated, stiff-collared, doing the more respon- sible jobs for less pay. I recognise not only the obvious – officer cadets come up to town to make trouble, streetwalkers those callow boys could never persuade – but also the odd ones, the missionary women collecting evidence to try and close the hall down, the Christian minister searching for fallen women to preach at and paw. But as for the women, all of them – stenographers, shop girls, nurses and teachers, mothers and others – have come here to alter their world a little tonight. Tonight, the audience is a little different; tonight Vesta Tilley is top of the bill.

In the long bar, famous all over the world, probably, for what they are doing, the women walk up and down in their fabulous clothes, displaying those waists which invite encircling hands. The manager smokes a cigar the size of a sausage, watching the women whose business so improves his own, if they are discreet, and the also-women (respectable, chaperoned) who know so little about the place they are in. There are boys there, too, displaying their brief perfection, dressed up to show off their bodies, without getting caught. From where I lounge, tucked in my corner, I witness it all, and the barmen, who hide their smirks behind vast moustaches and wear stiff aprons long to the floor, bring me my hock and seltzers on the house, in between serving champagne, burgundy, gin.

'Crowd,' one of them says, nodding at his clients.

Yes, indeed it is a crowd; some promenade up and down the room, some cluster in groups, in twos, some hurry past, eyes averted, to their seats. The gentlemen are very sleek this evening, very tailored, perhaps on their mettle against competition from the stage. The ladies, I think, are also making – shall we say – a special effort. I flatter myself that I can even tell which have seen the London Idol before, and which have not. Those in the know are expectant, anticipating some extra-ordinary occasion, and their excitement may be repressed, but it shows. The others, who are here for the first time, have caught the atmosphere but are still cautious, and hold back a little, until they can see this thing with their own eyes.

Later, I will go upstairs, away from the well-to-do throng who visit the music hall as one diversion of many, to sit with the gallery girls who scream adoration for their hero, whose entertainment this is. Here, there's no ragged, fried-fish-munching mob; the prices keep them out. But the crowd in the gods is raucous enough to make the ladies in their evening gowns feel that they're doing something rather risky, and the young men think themselves real dogs tonight. My place is up there, watching with my own kind squashed in on a bench, rather than sprawling here in the long bar, a witness from the other side of the tracks.

Ella sails up, rests on the bar beside me; her stays creak slightly, but the expanse of bosom she suddenly exposes as she leans forward across the countertop causes a small sensation opposite. 'Wotcher, John', 'Wotcher, El', we grunt together. She tells me of the talent here tonight; Ella knows everyone by sight and name, though few of them might recognise her face. *Tatler*, *The Lady*, *Queen* and other gossip manuals keep her well-informed about people to whom she'll never speak.

'It's a gay crowd tonight,' Ella remarks, downing her port with unladylike ease.

'Not your scene then, darlin',' I drawl, discouraging.

'I dunno.' She whisks round, leaning her elbows backwards on the bar, and pointing her décolletage at me. 'There's a few here I wouldn't mind a try with.'

I roll my eyes, and tell her she's a flirt, which is the most polite phrase I can find. She points out various women of a type that even she can recognise in public; an arty pair in beads and woven dresses who cross the room pointedly arm in arm, a group of sporty-looking bluestockings who must be at the university, all in their boyish coats and rakish hats. Then there's a pair to make the heart beat faster, all lace-encased curves and inviting flesh. They've got a young man with them, camouflage which prevents Ella knowing what they are, but I have noticed how they look at me (somewhat uncertainly). But her attention's soon back on the men; she likes them with narrow hips and wide shoulders, and she laments how many here are on the game themselves, or on the lookout for another boy.

Later still, when the show is over, I'll go backstage, away from all this bright light into the dim, unglamorous corridors to find my girl. Lily is in the chorus, but she's not one of those who shows her legs off but whose face is vacant. Lily's curvaceous, but she keeps her clothes on (and, incidentally, she can sing and act). The others know she's, as they say, 'got serious', and so they cover for her to the boys who clamour for the actresses' favours. In the days I was on the boards myself, before I took to doing the act full-time, the chorus dressing room was out of bounds, which was supposed to keep things very proper. Now I can wander in and prop myself on Lily's dressing table to watch her dress, make up and do her hair. It's a performance which I much prefer to the sweet sentimental stuff they sing onstage, and private, too. She's too good to me; Ella said at once 'She'll soon sort you out, handsome,' and so she does, divinely. It's a bargain to suit both.

A bell sounds shrilly, people start to move, the orchestra can be heard tuning up. There are a lot of acts before La Tilley, but still many take their seats, in a spirit of happy expectation. Ella's still rattling on about Miss This and Lady That, heiresses, honourables; all stuff that's tedious beyond belief, even if the women themselves might interest me.

'Who are those two, then?' I ask, to test her knowledge.

This couple, sweeping in when the place is half empty, can't help making an entrance. The older woman is a mellow beauty of the voluptuous, blown-rose, *grande dame* type, whose deportment denies the thought of hurry. Her companion is a good few years younger, perhaps in her mid-thirties, handsome and tailored (as much as a conventional woman can be), very much the escort. This woman makes me think of how I used to be; she's got her hair up in a way that makes it look as short as possible, she moves as definitely as men can, and yet there's still something unfocused about her appearance. Evidently, the thought of being late has catapulted her into a rage; the older woman pats her arm, placates her, the usher soothingly conducts them in (to best stalls seats, of course).

'Mrs Moncrieff,' Ella tells me, triumphantly, 'society opera singer. And her companion, Miss Neville Gray, the poet, whose friends call her Freddie.'

(This was before, need I say, when Gray was neither famous nor infamous, before those books and that play, before the trial and the wife-stealing, before she became one of our crucified martyrs, our own icon and idol, the mirror in which we saw our ideal selves. This was when she was just a gentleman-in-waiting, *cavaliere servente*, spoilt boy in skirts, still learning her craft in more ways than one. Her name meant nothing to me then, although already I could see her potential, even imagine her committing the playboy enormity of trousers.)

'They're *not* mother and daughter,' Ella adds, meaningfully.

'I hardly thought so.'

Both belong to the Vesta-virgin category, I decide, though with the older one it's hard to tell, as that rich, indolent manner quite disguises any real emotion.

While the first acts (magicians, jugglers, comics, *poses plastiques*) all do their thing, Ella and I stay chatting in the bar, half-listening to the music, applause, patter. For the chorus numbers, I go hurrying through with all the lads and lean against the stalls' flock-papered wall to hum the chorus, raise my glass to Lily, and shout 'huzza' when they're done. I notice those two women, Ella's names, sitting close by me in their pricey seats; the matron's velvet stole has slipped away from her smooth, rounded shoulders, and her squire is all attention in draping it back. Their little double act amuses me, so I'm attending when the music changes to announce Vesta Tilley's imminence. There's an influx of audience, preparatory murmuring, the two stretch up to see better, and stay there. The intro is repeated twice, three times, before the London Idol loiters on, strolls downstage and acknowledges the pandemonium her appearance causes by tipping back her bowler, touching her cane up to its curly brim. I've seen our Tilley many, many times; I know the tricks, I do the walk myself, and yet I'm floored this time and every time. So the effect she has on the unwary is simply staggering. Mrs Moncrieff – so far as one can tell behind the perfectly-composed facade – is quite amused, but also rather shocked, perhaps can't help but disapprove unladylike behaviour. Her young acolyte is struck by lightning; she stares up at the stage hungrily, lips parted, yearning, her eyes burn with storm electricity. (I observe this by watching from my vantage; both are far too discreet to be apparent.) It isn't often that you catch that moment; the seminal, the inspirational, the visible imagining, the spark caught and passed on.

(Whenever I saw her picture in the paper later, with the Eton crop, the monocle, the heavy masculine jewellery and heavy masculine smile, the immaculate tailoring, I would be transported back to that moment. I would remember seeing her stir in her chrysalis, so long before the dapper butterfly emerged, the wingless thing already desiring to fly.)

Offstage, Vesta's afraid of her own power and tries to separate her life and art, but here and now she's revelling in it. In her stride, she holds the perfect balance between the young man she appears to be, and the young woman we all know she is. And she can meet my eye unflinchingly, and wink at me in a comradely way, although what I do frightens part of her. Yet she flirts with the women in the audience, teases the men, accepts the fans' thrown tributes, and all the while continues her great act. It's just so funny. The thing with Vesta is, she looks exactly like a boy – too handsome, maybe, and far too well-dressed – but as the critics say, an ideal boy. Except she isn't, and we know she's not, so every step she takes is wild transgression, utterly delightful. She's got all the gestures, swagger, gait, off to perfection; just an edge of satire, but otherwise convincing. The songs she sings are naughty, like this evening, it's 'Oh, you girls, you wicked young girls, why can't you try to be good?' We're not in any doubt about what she means. And, strangely, all the women watching her not only melt over this handsome sprig; they also envy her, and want to be her, to emulate her freedom. I don't believe that suffragettes wear ties because they think them prettier than lace; those women are usurpers, and good luck to them.

I watch Vesta's act as the fellows do, roaring with laughter at my vanity when she peacocks about in her posh suit, flicks dust that's not there off her shiny boots, polishes up her nails on her lapel or straightens her tie knot admiringly. But I'm remembering that she is a woman, too, when she's kissing their fingers in the front row, sipping out of some girl's glass from the boxes, yelling 'You too, darlings!', back at the gods, when the gallery girls scream down 'We love you!'. It's a strange mix which is intoxicating.

Encore after encore – no, take it from the top. So, she's on; she strolls down to the footlights and poses, for us to all appreciate her costume. She speaks her introduction, quells the laughter, struts back and forth in time to the music, and when she sings, she can play with the rhythm, drag the words out long against it then belatedly rejoin it and sweep into the next chorus, caught up. There's a singalong, pub-piano jolly, but she can stop the applause with a gesture, or bring us in on cue with one raised eyebrow. Encore after encore is roared for, given, until at last they bring the curtain down, leaving us breathless with her energy.

As the house lights come up, I see my youthful other self in the audience, still transfixed, staring ahead without hearing her companion, and smiling fiercely, privately. Suddenly, she turns and begins talking, with excitement, waving her hands about elaborately. I see that her experience with Vesta has already begun to change her, just as people so quickly assume their lovers' mannerisms. And I remember, oddly vividly, those moments when everything's changed for ever, for the better, by some silly song or strange work of art which alters the vision. (Though look where that's got me.)

There is nothing worse than a departing audience, still exalted with the performance, but falling since it's ended. I get out of the way before they begin their long shuffle past. Fortunately, I don't need to annoy the people waiting outside the stage door by being let in, while the top-hatted men with their flowers try to bribe the porter, or bluster their way to the front, and the vast silent groups of girls just stand, clutching their tributes for their favourites. No, I slip through the little door, disguised so that only its edges show through the wallpaper mask, in front of which an usher always stands, his uniformed chest hiding even the small 'No Admittance' sign. Beyond it is the familiar corridor, a narrow passageway between two worlds, dully glowing with artificial light. The floor and walls to halfway up are glossy dark green, ceiling and upper half egg yolk, or nicotine cream, its length punctuated with red sand-buckets. It smells of bleach, and slopes slightly downhill. As I make my way swiftly along towards my desired destination, somebody calls 'Excuse me!', with the haughty manner of the most privileged class, meaning 'I say, you, come here at once!'. The noise still echoes slightly as I turn, to see Miss Gray the poet there behind me, materialised within the private door. Then, mistaking me for a gentleman, she asks a shade less superciliously, 'Is this the way backstage?'

I bow, say yes, return towards her along the dim tunnel, crossing through pools of light and uneven shadow. I do not tell her that there's no admittance this way for the audience; the rules do not apply. She's carrying, awkwardly, a large bouquet of quite exquisite flowers.

'Are those for Miss Tilley?' I ask, amused.

'Why, yes. My companion sent her a note, and she invited us to her dressing room. Can you direct me?'

'Certainly,' I say. 'With pleasure. What about the other lady? Is she on her way too?'

'No, she has asked me to deliver her apologies; she has a headache.'

I wonder which of them wanted to send the note, to go backstage; not the *grande dame*, I guess.

'Well, I can show you the way,' I tell her, reassuringly. 'I'm going there myself to call on someone. I know Miss Tilley; I can introduce you.'

She considers this, decides not to take umbrage, strides confidently towards me. It is odd, how little sound reaches into this place, and footfalls sound loud in the corridor. We introduce ourselves, quite formally, despite the unconventional situation – although that does not seem to bother her – and turn to walk towards the backstage door. I think it's when I grin at her, unguardedly, she really sees me. It's like the recognition scene in all the best old-fashioned pantomimes; she steps back half a pace, eyes widening, claps one hand to her face, opens her mouth to speak, but can say nothing. (Except in this instance she doesn't then embrace me, exclaiming 'My long lost brother!') This can be very awkward, as I know from past experience. There is utter silence, and I wait, just looking at her. Sometimes they laugh, or slap me, cry, or try and fall into my arms; you just can't tell. After a long considering pause, she smiles, with all the charm that was formerly lacking.

(And that smile, the memory of her happy acceptance of her fate at this accidental annunciation was what made me, ever after till today and beyond, wish her well when she stepped out to confound the disapproving world in her glamorous drag, as polished as Tilley – or me.)

'This has been an extraordinary evening,' she says, as if to herself, and then laughs. 'A night of wonders and revelations.'

'You've never seen Miss Tilley's act before?' I enquire, gently.

'No, never. Nor anyone like – do you – are you ... ?'

'I've been in the business a long time now.'

'I envy you that. And I adore the theatre.'

We're walking onwards, slow and deliberately as in a dream, when she abruptly stops, and takes me by the arm.

'Did you say you were going to call on someone?'

'Yes, Lily, my girlfriend; she's in the chorus.'

'Please give her these flowers, if you think she'd like them. I think I needn't meet Miss Tilley now, although she was – magnificent.'

'An eye-opener, as she herself would say.'

We tussle for a moment with the flowers, both equally inept, and when I've overpowered them we shake hands, both equally sincere. Then, shy again, she almost runs back to the audience-world of ordinary life, leaving me to pass in the opposite direction. But she pauses while still in sight to call 'Thank you and – good luck!', bowling the words along at me, like the principal boy throwing pantomime sweets. I wave.

Green Card
Alix Baze

From the balcony of our third-floor apartment I photographed the snow covered yard, the ice threatened trees. The balcony was made of timber – pale blue – sheltered from grey skies beneath a paint flaking roof. Vines severed from their roots would not give up the corner joists. A stairwell provided a pass to this veranda, a way of access to our routinely unlocked kitchen door. That winter Yvonne and I shovelled and salted the snow for sure footing.

The days were short. One evening I was scrubbing a baking tin, trying to remove a burnt crust with a scourer. I heard Yvonne's tread on the stairs – feet scrunching snow that salt couldn't melt. I submerged the tin into hot milky water, wiped wet hands on my jeans and rushed to my easy chair by the stove. I sat cross legged and waited. Through the insulating plastic cover over the screen door I saw a fuzzy outline of Yvonne appear, saw the shape of her smile as her face moved in closer to the light. The screen swung wide and fell to rest against her blue suede coat. She opened the inner door and stamped her feet. Snow pieces flew and melted on the warm hardwood floor. 'I smell scones,' she said, pulling her hat off with one hand and tugging at her scarf with the other.

I stood up to pick out two fruit scones from the cooling grid, the biggest ones, that promised the most sultanas. I felt Yvonne's hands on my waist. 'I wish you didn't have to work,' I said. 'You should be able to stay home and study.'

Yvonne kissed the back of my neck. 'It's an investment.' She pulled away from me to go sit by the stove. I followed carrying the scones on a plate. We sat and broke open our cakes. Steam twisted out. 'I can manage to do both right now,' she said. 'You'll be working soon enough. Then I'll be a student housewife for a while. I'll kinda like that.'

I smiled. 'But I wish I could contribute now.'

'I'm just glad we're together.' She popped a morsel of scone into her mouth. 'We're lucky your university is allowing you to finish the degree here in the States.'

'True. Anyway, next summer I'll have my master's, and still about three months left on the tourist visa to look for work. Then you'll see – I'm gonna treat you right.'

'You already do,' she said, munching on the last of her scone.

During the frozen months that followed, I worked steadily on a portfolio for my course. In the evenings Yvonne and I would sit by the stove and talk. Legs outstretched, toes flexing, we caressed warmth, felt it grow and fill our home. When the kitchen door was opened an escape of heat was to be expected; we even welcomed the regular blasts of icy air that rushed in to balance the pressure. They reminded us that we were in New England. They also heralded the arrival of friends – pot luck dishes in hand, pets in tow. When one person came, invariably, others would follow.

Our refrigerator was loaded; our food cupboard stocked. Outside, close to the stairwell and elevated by a wooden chair, a five-litre wine box constantly chilled. My slippered feet made imprints in fresh falls of snow as I drew Mountain Chablis to offer guests. Inside, Yvonne entertained with stories, many from her life before we met – like how she'd worked on a cruise boat in Alaska and saw the arcs of humpbacks that rose and plunged to smash the waters with the turn of their tails; or how she'd hitchhiked once from Maine to Florida, and how during that week she'd seen pine trees laden with snow, cherry trees in full blossom, orange trees ripe with fruit.

Days passed. Blizzard after blizzard piled upon the house, made Inuits of us in a high-rise igloo. Snow shifted outside, buried familiar objects, created new landscapes with every storm. During the night when the heating was off, tiny crystals of snow, hounded by the wind, would find their way beneath the kitchen door. By morning a glistening range of melded flakes stopped the gap. When the days began to lengthen, icy rains fell, encasing all things with liquid glass. Standing on the balcony in boots and pyjamas, Yvonne and I marvelled at the scene. She draped her arm around my shoulders. Below us berries displayed on bushes like glacé cherries on silver cocktail sticks; trees hung like huge chandeliers, branches tinkling with each breeze. To see our breath we huffed onto the air. Vapours from our hot lungs materialised like ghosts – translucent – only to vanish.

In the spring I made a birdseed tray: one weekend I salvaged wood – a plank of soft pine and a strip of decorative beading – from a dumpster in front of our neighbour's house. I took it to our balcony and went inside to find Yvonne. She was tidying up the mayhem of clothing in her closet. I sat on the bed as she gathered bundles of thick flannel shirts, fleece socks and pullovers, and tossed them into a trunk. She closed the lid and pushed the trunk beneath her row of hanging clothes. Then she sat down next to me and linked her arm through mine.

'And what are you up to?' she asked.

'Gonna build that ritzy bird restaurant you've been going on about.'

She gave a squeal and hugged me.

I shooed her out of the apartment, watched as she trotted down the stairwell. When she reached the corner she glanced back. I waved and she was gone.

The beading I'd left on the balcony was longer than I needed. I made marks on it with a pencil where I wanted to make my cuts. The wine box chair became my work bench. I placed the timber on the chair and my foot on the timber to use my body weight as a brace, the way I'd seen my father work when I was young. I remembered how he'd lift a plank to eye level and stare along its surface to make sure it was true, or run his hand over the grain to feel for imperfections. As I sawed through the thin strip of wood, dust sprinkled downwards, forming tiny hills on my boot toes, small drifts against tools. It buried nails and fell between the slats of the deck to the balcony below. Our porch smelled like a lumber yard. When four lengths of beading were cut to size, I tacked the decorative strips into position to form a brim around the pine base.

I cleared my carpentry tools and swept the dust. I wanted clean space in which to paint. Flattened pizza delivery boxes were ideal to protect the balcony floor. There were some paint tins in the basement, oil-based colours. Yvonne had already selected her favourite. I painted the seed tray. Scary red. Red was left over, so I gave some coats to a metal flowerbox lying empty in a corner. I propped the seed tray and the metal box on some wood supports to dry. On one of the supports, dangerously close to the wet lip of the metal box, was an ant. I brushed it away. The ant landed close by, began to crawl back towards the support. I flicked it, off the balcony and into the garden.

In late sunshine I leaned against the aluminium siding of the house, red on my hands, arms and clothing. I heard a door open onto the veranda of the apartment below ours – 'Hey, could you use a beer?' Yvonne called.

Next morning the paint was dry. After bagels and cream cheese, Yvonne helped me position a step ladder so I could fix the seed tray to a weathered beam, to overhang the garden like a ledge. When the seed tray was in place she filled it with corn flakes. 'Till we get some seed,' she said.

We went downstairs. I took the flowerbox to the yard; Yvonne went to borrow some trowels from our first-floor neighbour. In the garden we filled the box with soil heavy with spring rain. Together, we carried it back up the stairwell, sideways like adventurous crabs. On the balcony we secured it to boards that jutted beyond the safety of the lattice guard rail. We wedged it between the wooden rail and a piece of leftover beading that we screwed into place, brown against red against blue. I looked at Yvonne, her earthy hair, flushed face and clear eyes.

'I suppose we should put some flowers in it now,' she said.

I glanced at my watch. 'We can still make the farmers' market if we hurry.'

We brought home petunia, lobelia, marigolds and pansies. We also brought back a weather gauge, tomato plants and sunflower seeds. We ate lunch then began the job of filling the flowerbox bed. Yvonne eased two or three lobelia out of a plastic cup, revealing a cone of entwined roots. 'These'll take well,' she pointed out.

When the flower bed couldn't fit more plants, we searched for other containers. We found an old earthenware pot and an array of baskets, buckets and pans. As I filled all these with soil, Yvonne filled them with plantlife, then transformed our balcony into a nursery. She moved the containers from this place to that, figuring out the best light or shelter. She spoke to the nurslings. 'This is your new home,' she'd say. 'You're part of our family now.' She gave me a list of duties as she organised. 'You should breathe on them sometimes when I'm at work – they like that – and sing to them. We'll water them together when I get home.' When she finished arranging, Yvonne swooped up the weather gauge from the deck and hung it from a small rusted hook twisted firmly into a rafter.

As spring progressed, the red liquid confined to the vertical channel of the weather gauge expanded and had no course but to climb the thermometer's scale. Soon we tore away the insulating plastic sheets from the windows and screen door.

Late April I mailed my completed portfolio to the university. The deadline wasn't until the end of May – 'Just in case it gets lost in the post,' I explained to Yvonne. Till my final results arrived there was nothing I had to do but enjoy the season.

Slurping hazelnut coffee, nibbling blueberry muffins, Yvonne and I moulded to our kitchen chairs. We watched as birds fed and flowers opened.

Summer came. At ground level, against the base of a corner beam was a heap of amber wood dust – like a tiny wheelbarrow load purposely tipped there. I passed this pile many times, noticed it on several occasions. It wasn't until I realised the dust heap had grown that I inspected its circumstances. About thirty centimetres above the heap was a cavity in the beam a little bigger than my fist. I peered inside. Splinters dangled from its walls. I investigated the other side of the timber. Higher up it looked corroded, full of small fissures. I stood on tiptoes to press with my thumb. It sank into the beam, fissures collapsing along a fault, wood crumbling. I began an exploration of the stairwell, discovered other areas had been excavated: a banister, a girder.

On the second-floor porch I spotted the culprits. Large black ants. They trooped. Woody loads held aloft. Dedicated lumberjacks. Ant traffic flowed steadily along a sunny floorboard, the loggers disappearing at each end of their road into cracks in thick supporting timbers. I knocked on my neighbour's screen door. There was no answer. I hung over the guard rail and shouted up – 'Yvonne! Come see this.'

Returning to the ant road, I crouched down for a closer view.

'What's up?' Yvonne asked, squatting next to me.

'Look,' I said. 'I think they're carpentry ants. You should see one of the foundation beams downstairs.

There's a huge hole where it's been eaten away.'

'Is that what they do? Eat wood?'

'I'm not sure. Maybe they take it apart for the hell of it. Some of the timbers are porous in places. You can almost squeeze them like a sponge.'

'Is that the ants too?'

I wanted to say yes, but when I thought about it, I wasn't sure. 'Whatever it is, the building isn't safe.'

'It's that slumlord of ours,' Yvonne said. 'She doesn't give two shits about this place. She should be made to fix this.'

'Yeah, I know. But there're advantages to being forgotten about. Remember when we asked her for a fence around the yard? After she installed the fence she put the rent up. We can't afford another increase.'

That evening we had a house meeting with our downstairs neighbours to discuss the ant problem over Margaritas. The meeting was held in the garden after a barbecue. Full, we sat around a white table that was strewn with soiled paper plates, opened sauce bottles, empty salad bowls. A fat black mutt stretched beneath the table. I rubbed my toes across his soft belly. He didn't move – replete with stolen treats. Our party of concerned co-tenants sipped on drinks Yvonne served in salt rimmed tumblers over crushed ice. After much drinking and deliberation this community reached a consensus: to have regular house meetings, and keep close eyes on ants.

Yvonne and I slept in late the next morning. It was a Monday. Vacation time spent at home was delicious on a week day. After we woke I got out of bed to make us tea. When I returned Yvonne had fallen back to sleep. I placed the two cups of steaming tea onto the floor and climbed between the bed covers. I lay my head on the pillow and studied her curling lashes, the way they grew fair at the ends. I fell asleep counting freckles.

That morning we took time: getting up, getting bathed, getting dressed, eating breakfast. While I enjoyed my third cup of coffee Yvonne went to check the post. She returned with one letter and held it out as she walked towards me. I put my coffee down and stood up to take the mail. I recognised the handwriting. University of Wales was stamped in red on the top left corner. My supervisor.

'Well? Open it,' Yvonne said.

I turned the envelope over and lifted the gummed flap. I read the note out loud. *Congratulations!* I grinned. *You've passed! It'll be a while before you're notified officially, but I know you're anxious to start job hunting. Do keep in touch and let me know how you get on. Regards to Yvonne.*

Gordon

'Well done!' Yvonne hugged me.

'This is fantastic,' I said, still within her arms. 'Now I can start sending out résumés.'

'And we can make plans for the future,' Yvonne added, releasing her embrace.

'I know! Well, almost. Don't forget, first I have to find an employer willing to sponsor me and wait for the temporary work visa to come through. But as long as I get that before my tourist stamp runs out I can apply for a Green Card. And when that's secured – love, I'm here to stay.'

Yvonne slapped her hands together. 'We should celebrate! Let's buy champagne – or go to the beach!'

I smiled. 'Let's do both.'

Across hot summer weeks we breezed in and out of our home. Sand shifted in thin dunes over the wood blocks of our kitchen floor. It gathered on the staircase, collecting in shallow bowls – depressions – worn into the steps by the tread of many climbers. It settled at the junctions in the lattice work, levelled the plugged spaces between the floor slats.

On days Yvonne worked she'd often pop home for lunch. She'd generally find me sat at the computer in the living room, researching employment opportunities or composing cover letters. The computer was six years old, but it had all the functions we needed and was dependable. Yvonne would use it in the evenings for her studies, so I'd save the task of filling in application forms till then.

One lunch time she showed up earlier than usual. She came in and kissed the top of my head – 'What'ya up to?'

'Organisation,' I said. 'Listing prospective jobs into categories: ones I'm fully qualified for; ones I don't quite match up to but could swing at interview; and ones asking for so many qualifications, maybe I'll be the only applicant. I'm focusing on teaching jobs within the university system. It's the sole area Immigration doesn't require the employer to prove they couldn't find an American to do the job.'

She kissed me again. 'You deserve a break. How about spending the afternoon with me?'

I leaned back to look at her face upside down.

She grinned. 'A meeting got cancelled. I've got the rest of the day off.'

'Great!' I straightened up. 'I'll finish here and be right with you.'

Yvonne went into the bedroom and I completed my last entry into the computer. After a few minutes she emerged wearing shorts and a T-shirt – 'See you outside,' she said. I shut down the Macintosh, then followed her onto the veranda.

The sun was high. My eyes adjusted to the balcony's gleam. A neighbour's cat was curled on our wine box chair. I scooped the animal up. He lay like heavy satin in my hands. I sat. Draped him across my lap. His fur was hot. He stretched, yawned, pushed himself off from my knees and padded down the stairs. I turned to watch Yvonne. She was tending our plants, removing withered flower heads to make way for new growth. Her hair fell forward. It shone with red in black. She reached down. Something on the deck attracted my gaze – a shoelace – around the base of a plant pot. A second glance confirmed the lace was a trail of large ants.

Standing up I tugged on Yvonne's shirt, then knelt for a closer look at the insects. 'I doubt the house will last another year.'

Yvonne rubbed my back. 'Have you ever seen the way ants behave if you break their scent trail?' It was an experiment she used to do as a child – see if the ants could find each other once separated. She picked up a small twig and dropped it gently mid ant flow. Ants stopped. Changed direction. But it wasn't long before they figured out a way over the obstacle. 'It's possible the ants have been here for years,' she said. 'Maybe they've just gone unnoticed till now. Really they've as much claim on the house as we have.'

I sighed. Perhaps she was right.

Our porch had developed into a gallery of colour. Two low deckchairs ensured we could fully enjoy the setting. Blue, violet and pink flowers cushioned boundaries, tumbled over the threshold of floorboards. Sunflowers raised heads above us. Marigolds grew in posies at our feet. Tomato vines provided a backdrop of green, fruit lazy in ripening.

At night Yvonne and I sat and watched the moon. Bugs sizzled in citronella scented flames as we held hands and listened.

Our summer ended.

The colour of the Fall is – principally – red, Yvonne wrote, overseeing the leaf scattered yard, the wind torn trees.

There are no more flowers, only foliage left on the plants. Some have died. The birds are getting expensive to feed; they're greedy and messy. The balcony is covered in wet grain.

It's getting cold. The skies are heavy and grey and I can smell snow in the air already. The plastic will need to go on the windows again soon.

I've signed up for another three classes. They seem complicated and dull. It's going to be a hard semester; and weird without you here.

Work is okay. I stay a little longer to get things done. When I got back tonight I tried to make macaroni cheese the way you make it, but the phone went and I burnt the bottom of the pan with the cheese sauce in it.

I'm not much company lately. When visitors call I don't have a lot to say. I'm preferring to be alone. I read your letters every night in bed. It calms me. Then I read them again at breakfast. I have a routine in the mornings. I get out of bed and turn on the stove and the percolator. Then, I draw the bath. By the time I've bathed, the kitchen has warmed. I get dressed for work and I sit in your seat by the stove. I drink my coffee, read your words and pretend that you're with me.

Dear Yvonne,

If I close my eyes I'm on our bed wrapped in you, both of us wrapped in the white glow of clouds through the skylight. Soon the clock will chime – we'll lie a while longer. Then you'll kiss me, and we'll make love.

I cannot comprehend we're compelled to live in separate countries – that to have remained with you would have been a crime. I knew if I couldn't find employment before my tourist visa expired I'd have to leave, but in truth the idea of separation, of being forced apart by a government, never was real to me. Even now, it's so hard to believe – that America dis-entitles us privileges taken for granted by so many other couples – that I'm denied the right to apply for immigration on the basis of our relationship, only because we are both the same sex.

You are my family. We should be able to build a life together, plant a garden, watch it grow beyond a year.

Sweet angel, don't give up. Perhaps I'll have more success finding work in the States from here. We must be patient, explore every immigration track. We will find our way through this, despite these laws. Our love is fluid, continuous – powerful like this ocean between us.

Yvonne, finish your degree. We'll work out the next step from there. I'll do everything possible to be with you legally. But if all else fails, if I have to marry a man – so they'll let me come home to you – I will.

The Hunger

Shameem Kabir

Part One: Vampire and Victim

I approached her as she stood outside the restaurant doorway. She looked at my red shoes and then she looked into my eyes. I said hello, shall we go in, and she said yes. I was aware of two men following us into the restaurant. A waiter came up to us and looked at all of us expectantly. 'A table for two, please,' I said, firmly, and he led us into the recesses of the room.

'That was easy enough,' she said, and then volunteered that this was her first time. 'Do you advertise often?' she asked.

'Not often,' I replied. I wanted to say, only when the hunger hits me, but I didn't. No point scaring her off. So I gave her the usual line, that it was a good way to meet women. The hunger was stirring. We both ordered meat. We began with aperitif.

She asked me if I'd had a good response to the ad. I said over a dozen letters. I didn't say she was number one on my list.

I'd known from her letter. Had I imagined that the ink was scented? Maybe I'd been prophetic about the hint of musk she carried. Her handwriting had betrayed her nervousness, firm strokes slightly jagged with tense anticipation. She had written a long letter, confessional but contained, as an act of bravado, a symbolic breaking off from her ex-partner, with whom she'd had an intense and traumatic time.

I saw the similarities at once. They were striking. But the most uncanny thing was that she had the same name as my own ex-lover: Alice.

(*Alice. She had left her because of the violence. Alice, who had devastated her.*)

I looked across at her, savouring the anticipated satisfaction of my appetite. She was everything I'd imagined, she even looked like Alice. Attractive, seductive, wearing red, the colour of rage. I wanted her. I suppose I'd decided what was going to happen that night before even meeting. I liked the appetite she brought out in me. And I wanted her to meet my hunger, to feed it.

The biriani arrived. Meat and fried rice speckled with scarlet, crimson and gold. The hunger had become unsettling by this time. We stopped talking to eat. The restaurant was playing Indian film music. I recognised the classic from *Awaara*, where Nargis is in a dream sequence. She sings 'Ghar Aya Mera Pardesi', my lover has come home. Then the sequence becomes a demonic song.

We wolfed the food down. She was drinking Beaujolais. I had opted for a Bloody Mary. We lingered over them, after the fullness of the food; red rich meat. The waiter brought us some segments from oranges which were blood-red and darkly delicious. I thought this was a good sign. They were quite succulent.

We looked at each other then. I invited her over to the flat, she agreed to come for coffee; we paid the bill, and left.

Coffee was a red herring, she really wanted alcohol. Her eyes lit up when I got out a bottle of red wine. I switched to cherry brandy, having run out of tomato juice.

I was expecting her to be a pushover, a drunken piece of flesh, and at that moment I was prepared to go along with that. I hadn't realised how much I'd like her, separately from anything sexual between us. She was drinking the wine as if it were water. But she seemed sober. No slurring, no slippages of words.

'Have you always lived in London?' she asked, and I liked the way she phrased the question. Not *Where do you come from?*, with its implication that I didn't belong here. So I told her, born in London, roots in India.

(*You have such an exotic background, Alice had exclaimed to her, as if the spanning of different continents were what made her a person worthy of Alice's attentions.*)

We talked about the usual things. I really did want to know something about her. That she was an object of my sexual appetite did not preclude my interest in her. I asked if she had ever gone out with a black woman before. She said she hadn't and that she would maybe correct this omission.

She told me a bit about her last relationship. She had had the same uncertainties, the same emotional battering and betrayal. Then she became reticent about the break-up. Boundaries.

We started talking about lesbian films. We'd both seen *The Hunger*, a lesbian vampire film.

'Do you remember the scene where Catherine Deneuve is at the piano, the two women are talking and the music is really seductive?' I asked.

She could remember the scene clearly. Susan Sarandon drinking sherry, the passion in both women's eyes.

'I thought it was charming,' I ventured, 'because we knew that they desired each other, and we wanted to see them articulate it.'

'Yes,' she said. 'We needed to see them articulate their lesbian desire by enacting it on the screen.'

We went on talking. We were still drinking. She had finished the bottle of wine and I was on my fourth cherry brandy. I felt warm towards her. So I was disappointed when she looked at her watch, said it was getting late. I didn't know if she was looking for a cue.

The hunger was back. 'You can stay the night, if you want,' I said, the calm in my voice belying the urgency I felt.

'I'm getting mixed signals from you,' she said. 'And that usually spells danger.'

'I do want you to stay,' I said. 'Does that clarify anything?'

'I'll stay,' she said.

Despite the danger we smiled. I opened another bottle of red for her. We went on drinking.

(*Alice got drunk and went out one night with a stranger, on a date. Everything changed after that. She could have taken the aggressive lovemaking that followed, that weight of a demanding and selfish desire, but it got serious when she began biting her, the occasional love bite, then worse, deliberately drawing blood on her lips.*)

The hunger began to rage again, when the clock struck twelve. It was a full moon. We went into the kitchen for a midnight feast and had a salami sandwich. She'd finished the second bottle of wine. I'd had half a bottle of cherry brandy. We were both stone-cold sober.

She kissed me in the kitchen. She put her hands through my hair and drew me closer. Our lips touched, fell into each other's fullness. Red on red. Our mouths meeting, open to the possibilities of pleasure. I was ready to devour her. The abandon ahead excited my senses.

We walked into my bedroom. I put on the orange light. She didn't want pyjamas. I let my gaze fall on her body.

She's so beautiful, I thought. She doesn't know what she's letting herself in for. We got into bed. I had to control myself.

(*She was in bed with Alice. It was their last time together. She had bitten into the flesh of her neck. Blood.*)

Part Two: The Turnaround

I can't go through with this, I thought. I turned around and faced the wall.

She lay on her back for a few moments, then she turned on her side and wrapped her body around me. The heat of her skin, the warm presence of her body, made me hot, anxious because desirous. I was afraid of losing control.

After a moment or two, when I didn't turn around, she asked, 'Is there something you want to talk about? I'm not tired.'

I knew she knew I was wide awake. 'I do like you,' I said. 'But I can't go through with this.'

'Have I said anything to distress you?' she asked.

'Not at all,' I replied. 'If anything I find you very attractive, it's just that . . .' I lapsed into silence.

She pressed her body against mine and I turned around to her. We needn't go all the way, I thought, maybe we could just kiss for a while. Our lips found each other and once again, I was swept into the dizzy softness of her mouth. As we kissed and touched I began to ache for the fullness of her body. She started to touch me more intimately, her hands moving across my back and down my body, her tongue becoming more demanding. My hunger for her was persuading me into going along with this, into facing the consequences later. After all, this was why we'd got together.

And then, just as desire seemed to sway me into giving in, the doubts returned, magnified by the fact that I liked her so much. No, I couldn't go through with this.

I went rigid. She noticed at once, and stopped. We lay there in the silent night, the orange light making us appear soft but sharp to the sight.

'You can talk about it, if you want,' she said. 'I'm a good listener.'

'You could be my therapist,' I said, wanting to keep things light between us.

She laughed, a bit grimly. 'I wouldn't be in your bed if I was your therapist. You'd be on my couch. With your clothes on.'

I laughed. 'Yes. I suppose there have to be rules for all relationships.'

Then she said, 'One rule has to be about honesty. So if you don't want to take this further, then okay, we can stop,

I can get a cab home. But if you want me to stay, you're going to have to tell me what's going on.'

'I do want you to stay,' I said, 'But I don't know where to start.'

'Okay, I'll start,' she said. 'You already know I liked your ad, that's why I wrote to you. When you called me I immediately liked your voice, the things you said. You sounded different. So I was looking forward to meeting you. I've not done this before, but I thought the way we set things up, you know, a Saturday night, meant that there was a chance that things could start up. I was open to that. I've told you some of what happened in my last relationship. I want to move on, and having a meaningful relationship with another woman will help me heal. I can't go on mourning the impossible. Anyway, I was hopeful about this evening. And I was pleased when you turned out to be real, not a cipher or an imitation. You're an original. I think you're intelligent, attractive, you're funny and serious at the same time in a way I find engaging. I want you.' She stopped.

She had just said everything I could want to hear from a woman I found attractive, sensual, desirable. It was a fantasy come true that she was expressing her desire for me so clearly, so unequivocally. But I know about the danger of fantasy becoming reality. And rather than be glad about the reciprocity of our desire, I felt the old dread lurking, ready to pounce out of its hunger for destructiveness. She was troubled by our encounter because she sensed there was a lot more going on. She was right. As she started talking again, I let my gaze fix itself on her features, and again I was conscious of her beauty.

She went on, 'About this evening, as you know, I was getting mixed signals. On one hand I could tell you wanted me, but I wasn't sure what for, I mean, I'm not into sex for the sake of it, it's got to be about mutual desire, about magnetism, and sex alone doesn't do that for me. So I've been curious about your intentions.'

I had to clarify what was going on. 'I did want us to have sex,' I said. 'It's all complicated by my previous relationship.' I paused, then rushed ahead. 'I haven't made love with a woman in three years. To tell you the truth, I'm terrified. I thought if I could just separate anything emotional from it, keep it something physical, then sharing sex wouldn't be so threatening. I thought that as long as I could pretend you were just a sexual object, it would make me forget how frightened I really am. But I find I do like you, I do desire you for who you are, not just for your body. That was a complication for me. I wanted sex, not feelings. I wanted pleasure without anything emotional attached to it.' I stopped. I didn't know how she'd respond. Would she run? I'd blurted out everything without sequence, but she wanted honesty, and that's what she was getting, with all its confusions and contradictions.

'Why do you need to separate sex from emotions?' she asked.

'I'd be in more control,' I said. 'I can't afford to get into something that leaves me defenceless. That's what happened in my last relationship. I'm still healing, even though it ended three years ago.'

'What happened?' she asked.

'Well, the relationship became . . .' I faltered, then I continued with a neologism, 'It was vampirific.'

'What do you mean?' she asked.

So I told her about Alice, about the biting and the blood. About the fantasies. I told her how my dreams had become haunted by vampirific images, of non-reflecting mirrors and the brandishing of crucifixes; how there had been corpses in my nightmares, carrion coming alive like something out of George Romero's *Night of the Living Dead*.

She asked me if I'd been sickened or seduced by these images. I said both; I'd been repelled but fascinated at the same time. She said I seemed to have issues that I'd like to bury but which were still alive for me. It was true. I hadn't worked out what Alice, my ex, had brought up for me. I had come to have a fascination for the forbidden. I was anxious that if I were to make love to a woman, or if a woman were to make love to me, I would lose control, I would want more, I would want the sex to be violent and demanding, not gentle and giving. Somehow this had all become tied up with my survival. My life seemed to be at stake.

She volunteered her opinion – generously, I thought. 'I'd say you have to work through different issues that you're collapsing together; issues to do with ambivalence about sex, fears of loss of control, confusing passion with violence, things like that. It's not impossible, you know. You can work it out.'

'I would like that,' I said. Then I kissed her. And then I took her to the edge.

Afterwards, we were talking again, it was one of those forever nights. 'Why vampires?' she had asked, looking at me quizzically.

'Return of the repressed?' I suggested, without thinking, then realised yes, that was why the myth of the vampire has such a hold over us. Like hunger, like desire, returning because irrepressible.

It was about two in the morning. We were hungry again. 'Hoummos?' I suggested.

'Too much garlic,' she said. We laughed and had taramasalata instead, with delicious baguette bread.

And then – it is later. We are in bed. Your mouth is on mine. You caress me. I have waited for this night for years, have wanted this, have waited for you to banish the spectre of my desire. I have been haunted, and now, you have come home. My lover has come home. Your lips leave mine, you descend to my nipples where they become full in your mouth, yes, I have wanted this for years. You move on, on and down, down to where I long for you. Wet and wanting, we impact, your tongue laps at me, lingering, I start to ache deep inside me, your mouth takes me in, closes, you lick me rhythmically, I go with these waves that are pulsing through me, then your mouth closes in again, your tongue becomes ferocious, insistent and alive the way I want it, I fall in with the sweeping as you take me, then the urgency increases, a new reel of sensation unfurls as unfolding you take me to abandon, your tongue moving me to the point of no return, and now I want you, I want you now as I go over the precipice of wanting nothing else, nothing but this deep drawing of me, I want to quicken and flower and, and, and yes, I cave in completely.

Afterwards, as we lay looking into each other's eyes, she said, 'We never did tell each other what we do. Will you tell me now?'

'I'm a writer,' I said. 'Will you forgive me if I record this evening on paper?'

'It depends on what you write,' she replied. 'Let's see.'

'What do you do, Alice?' I asked, addressing her by her name for the first time.

'I'm a linguist,' she said.

We laughed. That night was sweet, as sweet as the blood-red oranges we'd had to eat.

One Night Wonder
Julie Clare

I love that first five minutes in a dyke club. I get there late. Coming in the door the fresh sweat and juice of a hundred women hits me. The beat's so loud it vibrates right up through the soles of my feet. I stand still, just for a few seconds, to soak up the music. At the bar I get an ice-cold bottle of beer. I find a place to lean back, chill out and breathe it all in. I take that first taste, where the liquid hits the back of my throat, resist the bubbles for a millisecond, then let it roll down like a roller coaster, and in my head I'm naked in a crashing waterfall. Oooooooh girl, I earned that beer.

Then I'm scanning the crowd, searching heat. I'm enjoying the shape of the bottle at my lips, the beer slipping down, and I'm looking, see what woman I'd like to warm my tongue against later on. I don't go for any particular type or look but even in a crowd I can see who I might move off my spot for. And I'm always straight with women – well, as straight as any woman born a dyke can be. I'm not looking for no relationship, no thank you very much. I did that meaningful thing a long, long time ago and I don't want to do it again. So I'm always up front and clear – what you see is what you get – one night only – take it or leave it. Lucky for me I got a good way to make sure no one feels too cosy. I always go to their place. I give them as much loving as I've got to give and I'm gone before morning. I don't sleep much anyway, but I never sleep out. I love women, every which way they want and every square centimetre of them. I just don't want to wake up and find they've set my place at their table and got me a pair of slippers, d'you know what I mean?

I'd seen Jackie around – she's hard to miss. Stunning to look at – hair so dark it's nearly black and cut really close to her head. Not many women have a face to carry that severe a cut, but she does – high slavic cheekbones and animal eyes, dark and deep enough to drown in. She's muscle and nerves and bone and she shoots through the place like an arrow. I watch women move out the way of her energy, but their eyes follow her. The word is that she always leaves you wanting more and those that like her say that's fair enough and those that don't call her a control freak. I think I could handle it. I followed her with an idle attraction at first but lately I've been feeling restless, needing a night of fire and fury, and I've tried to catch her eye. Last Christmas I got one of those little spinning tops in my cracker – the sort that looks still when you spin it but it's actually whirring round like crazy on the spot. And when that brought her image flashing to my mind I knew that I would ignore any warnings and risk getting a little scorched for a night, maybe even welcome it.

I spot her four minutes into the search. She's dancing with a gentle, way sexy rhythm, real deliberate. I can only see her from the back but it's a hell of a view. Her hips are moving like they're riding the waves on a warm rocking ocean and they're practically screaming come here and hold me. Her jeans are tight over all her curves and I'd guess creating quite a pressure between her legs too. She's got her arms swirling slowly above her head and they're bare, bold and strong. Some kind of Celtic tattoo on one arm makes patterns in the air. This woman knows how to make a space and fill it full up. She's dancing by herself, with herself and for herself. As I'm watching her I can feel desire start to spiral up inside me and I want her skin on my skin, her salt on my tongue. I put my bottle down and move closer to wait. Wouldn't do to interrupt this dance. As I reach the floor I catch sight of these tiny freckles on her arms and I want to rub my face against them. I can see all the lights reflecting off this big mess of curly auburn hair when she turns and sees me watching her. I give her my best smile and she winks at me. Go, girl, go...

'You are one very cool dancer.'

'Thank you,' she says and smiles a really warm smile.

'Can I get you a drink?'

'Vodka, please.'

'With anything – tonic or something?'

'I don't mix spirits. Just ice, please.'

Something's beginning to tell me this woman doesn't mess around and I like that.

As I pass her the drink I catch a strange scent, like some kind of herb or earth or something. And I get a second's flash of black satin and creamy white cleavage that starts my heart pumping overtime.

'One vodka...sorry, I don't know your name.'

'Thanks. It's Al.'

'Is that short for Alison, Alice?'

'Alexandra. As in Princess.' She smiles again, shrugs and raises one eyebrow. I steady myself, inside and out. It's going to be a good night.

'I'm Jackie.'

'I know you are...And I know the score.' She's still smiling and looking right in my eyes and I feel the pulse of desire beating really strong.

'And is the score okay with you?'

To answer she slides the fingers of her hand between my fingers, lifts our hands and squeezes them together into a tight fist.

'Let's go,' I say, lust stabbing me hard inside.

*

Outside the air feels clean and surprisingly warm for March. I open the back door of the cab and we sit close to each other. I'm not sure if she knows the driver but they seem pretty friendly. While she's leaning forward chatting to him I've got my hand under her clothes just stroking the base of her back. She's got a gorgeous hollow that I'm tracing lightly with my fingertips and I'm looking forward to lifting the tiny hairs there with my tongue. Her skin is soft and warm and in a few minutes she sits back against me, slightly turned away. We're not saying anything, not with words anyway, but I feel her body arch towards me and she begins stroking my hand with her fingers and it's totally electric, like there's an invisible thread from her fingers pulling on my cunt. We're already breathless by the time we arrive at her place.

It's a sweet little terraced number, real old Yorkshire blackened stone. The street is quiet, not surprising for one in the morning. She opens the front door then turns and begins to kiss me, pulling me inside at the same time. There's a low light and all I can see is her hair as she stands against the slammed door and drops her keys with a clatter on the wooden floor. So, no cup of coffee, no getting-to-know-you talk then. My hand comes up to her face, holds and caresses her as we taste each other. That same herby smell is pulling me closer to her. I brush the back of my hand against her forehead and gently begin stroking her hair back from her face. It's amazing – there's so much of it you'd think it's tough and wiry, but it isn't at all, it's baby soft and it makes me want to hold her safe against me. But she's a woman who takes her needs seriously and she is hot, hungry as a wolf. I push up under her T-shirt and stroke my appreciation along her sides. Her tongue grows more urgent in my mouth, and she presses me into her. I can feel her need through two layers of denim and pull away to look at her. Her pupils are wide, unashamed, and her lips are wet. I touch them, light as an insect wing, and something sad flashes past in her eyes and she closes them. She breathes deeply and then catches my finger between her teeth and bites hard. She opens her eyes and looks right into mine, unzips her jeans and puts my hand there. She is dripping full of juice and pulls my fingers inside her in a second. All the while her eyes are open and holding my gaze as she thrusts onto my fingers. A low noise begins somewhere inside her belly and begins to escape. I am drawn into her orgasm, see it in her eyes as her lids flutter and say, hey, watch me come. And I do, in glorious technicolour.

She falls forward into my arms and I hold her while her heart slows. The weight of her there is wonderful. Her hair is tickling my neck and I feel light, like I'm kind of floating. When she surfaces a few minutes later her face is flushed and she is only half embarrassed . . .

'Ooof, it's hot in here,' she mumbles. 'I need to open a window.' She's unsteady and pulls her jeans up as she walks. As I turn around I clock the room for the first time. Jesus H Christ on a bike. The whole place is jam-packed full of plants and the walls are ten different shades of blue. It's a crazy jungle kaleidoscope and it freaks me out a bit. Al begins to chuckle.

'I guess it takes some getting used to . . . I, well, people . . . I haven't had guests for a while and I forget . . . '

'It's cool, unusual, but cool,' I reply, feeling anything but cool.

'Look, I'll put the kettle on . . . It's . . . I . . . Take your coat off for God's sake, please.'

I do, and things go from bad to worse. I open what I think is the cloakroom door and see a whole cupboard full of tools. And I don't mean DIY either. There's huge long twisty metal things and helmets and sharp hooky spiky stuff and two chainsaws.

'I'm a mad axe-murderer in my spare time,' whispers Al behind me, and I jump a mile.

'I'm sorry, shit, I'm not doing well with the hostess thing am I?' she says. 'I'm a tree surgeon. Really.'

There's a long pause.

'Is that better or worse? And what the hell is this?' I ask, pulling out a very scary looking thing twisted like a giant corkscrew.

'It's an auger. It's for collecting a core of wood – for ageing a tree or examining it.' She's using a dead reassuring voice but I don't know if it's working. I sink down into her sofa to recover as she goes to the toilet.

When she returns she kneels between my legs and takes my face in both her hands.

'Are you okay?' she asks. I look at her steadily.

'You have the most perfect eyebrows I've ever seen. Yes, I'm okay.'

I run my tongue lightly under them and kiss the tiny lines at the corner of her eyes. By the time my lips reach the pulse flickering at her neck I can feel her relaxing again and I lift her onto my lap. She wraps her legs round me and squeezes me with strong thighs. I rest my cheek lightly against her breasts. I want them and she knows it. She lies me down on the sofa and sits on top of me and laughs. She's teasing me with her bold blue eyes as she unbuttons her shirt very, very slowly. Then we are kissing and licking and sucking any flesh we can find on each other and bits of us keep disappearing down the sofa cushions. I'm feeling her desire grow and grow and I love that need and I feed it as long as I can. When I know the ache in her is balancing on the edge between pleasure and pain I curl round behind her and fuck her very slowly with one hand as the other reaches round and gently strokes her clitoris. She lets go of her orgasm with a roar that's half joy and half rage.

We are still until her trembling stops and then she turns to me.

'I want to show you something...Can I?' She's hopeful and I hear myself agree.

'Okay, put your clothes back on...Do you want a waterproof or a hat or anything?' I think of what my mate

Sue would say if word got out that I'd worn a bobble hat and shake my head. She dresses quickly, brisk and practical.

'Come on, it'll clear our heads,' she says, and closing the door behind her she takes my hand. I don't do holding hands but somehow it's all right and we head up an alleyway. Now, I'm fit – I work out three or four times a week – but Al can really move fast and what with the lust and alcohol as well I just keep up with her. Plus she knows the way and as we jump over a gate into a field I give in and let her lead me. The grass feels spongy and the night isn't dark at all, more purple than black really. The moon is full bellied, nearly round. It's dead quiet too and I feel a bit like I'm on another planet. I think my mind drifts off somewhere, half of me enjoying the space and the other half not believing I'm walking anywhere in the middle of the bloody night, when all of a sudden we stop.

'This is my girl. She is without doubt the most beautiful for miles around. Look.'

I look. The trunk is pale grey and wide, looks solid and strong. It towers above us like a huge pillar. Halfway up there is a cluster of knobbly lumps, about eight or nine of them. They look like adolescent breasts, just beginning to grow. Further up the trunk are scars where branches have been cut off or fallen. There are swollen oval-shaped wounds I want to touch but they are too high. The branches are long and silver and powerful. I wonder if I've ever really seen a tree before.

'She is magnificent isn't she?' murmurs Al. I nod slowly. 'She's a beech tree, about 150 years old. Been around a long time, haven't you old girl? And you're looking good on it, aren't you gorgeous?'

I worry for a moment about being alone with a woman who talks to trees but then I can't resist feeling the bark. Its smooth, though tiny ridges scratch lightly on my skin. Al skips around the trunk and all I can see of her is two hands waving. I stand right up to the tree and our hands just reach each other around the width of it. My face is against the bark, feeling the cool cracks and creases, and my hands are warm in Al's. I guess hugging trees is okay and I'm peaceful for a while.

The next thing I know Al is behind me and I can feel her all the way along my body, especially her breasts below my shoulder blades. Her tongue grazes along the hairs on my neck and I'm suddenly craving her. As I try to turn she stops me and puts my hands above my head, holds them there against the bark. She carries on licking and kissing my neck and I can feel her hips pushing into me and it's driving me crazy. I see her left hand over mine and the strength of it tightens the knots in my stomach. Al suddenly lets go of my hands, turns me round to face her. She licks my lips, catches my bottom lip between her teeth, strokes me with her tongue. She unzips my jeans so slowly I can hear the tiny clicks of the metal teeth. As she slides her finger over and over my silky wetness I can feel the springs inside me unwinding. I rock onto her fingers and I can smell the tree and the earth. I lift my shirt. She circles my nipple with her tongue and then brushes her cheek gently against it, over and over again. I throw my head back as I come and the pattern of the branches and the stars above me make a pretty awesome backdrop. Some time passes with the lightest of breezes wafting Al's hair to my neck.

'Hey, you're shivering,' Al whispers and that's when I realise that I'm freezing and my whole body begins to shake. 'Time to get you inside, bit early in the year for moon-bathing, you know.'

I give her a piggyback some of the way but I still can't warm up. Inside the house Al runs into the bathroom and turns the tap on then runs back in and pulls my top off. I realise it's damp and sweaty and wonder if that's why I'm so cold. Al rubs her hands really fast up and down my arms. She throws her own shirt off, flings it on the floor along with the black bra and, holding me against her, rubs the sides of her hands hard up and down my back. It's like little trickles of burning lava on my back and her warm-blooded full breasts on my front and it's a shame the bath is running because I could just stay standing there.

I get in the steaming water and lower myself under so just my nose is showing and tingle all over. As I thaw I wonder if I'll get ill from all this ice and fire, and decide it's worth it if I do.

Al comes in to see if I want a hot drink. She's wearing her jeans but her breasts are still bare and I try and think of lots of reasons for her to come in and out like that because she looks so damn sexy. She brings lemon tea and while I'm sitting waiting for it to cool down she fills a huge jug with hot water and stands up and pours it over my head, again and again. It's heaven, water cascading on to me, and the movement of her arm lifting her breasts above me. Then she's telling me about her trees and asking me about my life as she washes me all over with soapy hands. And I'm getting this longing for her to lie on me in the bath, not for sex, but just to hold her in this warmth. So she does get in and when her hair is wet her head is actually very small and delicate and it fits neatly at my shoulder. We talk and kiss and hold until the water's tepid and she says she's hungry.

Jackie is everything I thought she would be. There aren't so many lesbians out there who really get high on making love rather than consuming love. There's a kind of reverence in her giving, a sense of worship that's like being honoured just for being a woman. It's very intense and very moving. And it lets me be myself. I expected all that from the fuss about her. But I didn't expect her to be fun somehow, and that's surprising. Bea, my beloved tree, liked her too and she's not easy to please. Of course what floored me was her vulnerability. It gets all my mothering instincts going as well as my sexual ones. So instead of feeling that light frisson of desire and excitement I've got the weight of a small cannonball in my pelvis. And there's not a thing I can do about it. Except stay strong enough to let her walk out the door.

So I'm wearing this cream towelling bathrobe and she's wearing a long violet T-shirt and she's searching the cupboards for something to eat while I watch from the kitchen table. It's not quite so bright or light in here but there's still a hell of a lot of plants. There's gentle music playing that I don't know – sounds Spanish or Latin American. She squats looking in the fridge for a long time and she's winding a wet curl round one finger and I can feel something in me splintering like wood.

'What about pancakes?' she asks.

'I haven't had pancakes since I was a kid, that'd be great.'

She sieves the flour into the bowl like she does a lot of things, I'm realising – from a height. There's a wide steel rim on the sieve that shines as the flour drifts down and it's like a kind of fairyland. She taps the egg hard on the edge of the bowl with one hand and splits the shell cleanly in two without pausing for breath. When she starts slowly mixing in the egg I can't bear it any more, the clinking of the whisk against the bowl and her breasts quivering under the T-shirt and knowing she's naked underneath it. Have you ever made batter with loving hands on your breasts? She does, lets me love her with my hands and face and tongue and she keeps right on whisking without losing the rhythm for a second as she turns the bowl. Then she picks up a cloth and covers it.

'That has to settle for half an hour. So what would you like to do?'

It's nearly six o'clock in the morning, which is around the time I like to leave but it's not over yet.

'Can I have the last dance?'

We hold each other carefully and move together, fragile at first. Then her hips begin to lead us and we're closer and fitting well with each other.

'What's that lovely smell on you?' She doesn't know what I mean and I try and describe it to her. She gets a tough-looking stalky plant and rubs it between her fingers.

'Is it this?'

'I think so...'

'Ahhh. That's rosemary...for remembrance...I use the herb a lot, and the essential oil. Or is it this?' She holds her other hand up and I can see the wetness glistening on her fingers and I know where it came from and it smells pretty wonderful too.

'Food – I need food,' she says and springs suddenly into action.

The smell of smoking oil fills the kitchen. I admire Al's strong hands as she flicks the batter into the pan without even a dribble escaping and then shakes it as it sizzles. When she tosses it so high it just misses the ceiling I feel my heart jump. She slides it onto the plate, hooks one arm around my shoulder.

'Lemon, madam?' I nod and she twists the lemon between her thumb and fingers and the juice shoots straight on to my pancake.

'Maple syrup? Organic Canadian actually.' A huge spiral of it appears on the pancake and then she's rolling it and telling me to enjoy.

The tart lemon and sweet syrup mingle in my mouth and the batter sinks to my stomach and soothes it. It's pure pleasure and I can't believe myself but I eat three, and so does she. After we lick the sticky juice from each other's lips I lift her onto my lap and enjoy the weight of her there for the last time.

'Thanks for a fantastic night. I think you're amazing,' I tell her, truthfully.

'It has been a wonderful night, hasn't it?' Her voice is quiet. 'I need to get horizontal now. And thank you. I wouldn't have missed it. I know you need to go – just post the key through the letter box okay?'

She kisses me lightly at the hollow of my neck and then she's gone. I sit for a while until I hear the bedroom door close and then I get up to leave. My feet won't move and I stay standing there. Al's body is pulling me like a magnet and I decide to wrap myself around her until she falls asleep. I don't usually want anything for myself but I do want that final comfort tonight.

There's a nightlight on in her bedroom, which is just as well or I might have trouble finding the bed amongst the chaos.

'Can I stay for a bit?'

She mumbles a yes and I get in. The sheets are cool and she is warm and I nestle in around her, my full stomach resting at the base of her spine. I slip one hand through the gap between her neck and the pillow and lay it on her breast. I'm gently caressing her thigh with the flat palm of the other hand, over and over. And then I do what I haven't done for fourteen years. I fall asleep with a woman.

And when I wake with empty arms and realise that the bed is cold and she has left, I do something else I haven't done in fourteen fucking years. I cry. Not a few tears, but huge sobs that make it hard to breathe. And I'm loud and I don't care and I don't stop until I am exhausted. I get up and go to the kitchen. There is a short note. It says:

Dear delicious Jackie,
I had something on this morning. If you feel like changing the rules I'll be back around noon with warm bread and open arms. If not, it's all right and I wish you everything you would wish yourself.
Al

I glance at the clock. It's ten to twelve. I feel slightly sick but I'm smiling. And I think I might stay.

The Patter
Mary Lowe

Her middle name was Fixit but everyone called her Zippy. Since the time she'd worked on her grandparents' farm in Scotland, she'd been hammering and chiselling, planing and mending. She was a dab hand with a soldering iron and could strip an engine in ten minutes flat. Her first sight of Bunty was on the Pagoda go-go dance floor. As she shuffled nearer, careful to avoid the clink, clink of steel-capped boots on lino, she imagined this graceful bird of a woman at home in a self-assembly kitchen making swans from napkins.

Bunty had been called Chloe in those days, but she'd always disliked the name – it sounded like something stuck in her throat. Two months in and Zippy was suggesting a new name. They were sorting through Bunty's old things; postcards, books, comics – there was a whole file of *Bunty*s going back to 1962. Bunty was grateful, it must be said, she'd never had such a masterful girlfriend, her track record was bound up with a succession of flakes with flabby forearms. In Zip she'd found her ideal woman. Strong, practical, with the best body this side of Hadrian's Wall.

Bunty on the other hand was thin and pale with a shock of peroxide hair and big blue eyes. A bit of a glamour puss with her carmine lipstick on. She fancied herself as a New Age truth seeker and had a penchant for women who were good with their hands. It was a match made in heaven. Everyone said. Bunty had the ideas and Zip delivered. Dado rails, skirting boards, electric sockets, dimmer switches – they sprouted like grass after a rainy day.

The rot started one Saturday afternoon when they were out shopping at The Mall. They'd spent two hours gazing at all things bigger and better under a plastic roof. It could have been snowing outside, they wouldn't have known. Trawling up and down the aisles with the uneasy feeling that they'd lost the car, forever parked in no-man's land between the Red and Blue Quadrant. They were about to go home, when Bunty wandered into Mothercare to buy a present for her nephew. Fifteen minutes later, she stumbled out to the bench where Zippy was waiting, her breathing shallow, her eyes glazed like maraschino cherries. She was in some kind of trance, a fainting fit. Zippy had a First Aid certificate and knew about giddy spells.

'Loosen your tight clothing,' she said. 'It must be the heat in here.'

But all Bunty could say was, 'Zip. I've decided. I want a child.'

And that was it. Words coughed up like a hairball as far as Zip was concerned. Amazing what a lack of oxygen does to the brain. Zippy bundled her out of the nearest exit into the fume-filled carpark. It took them a full half-hour to find the car but eventually they reached home and Zip ran Bunty a bath, her cure for all ailments.

'Take it easy,' she told her. 'You'll feel better tomorrow.'

But a dull ache settled in the pit of Zip's stomach that deepened whenever Bunty broached the C-word. Children had no place in Zippy's life. She'd never liked them, not since the time a six-year-old had tried to scratch its name on her newly installed fireplace. She'd tried to reason with Bunty; there was the financial aspect to consider, the time commitment, the effect of greasy marks on their smoked glass coffee tables. There was nothing positive about the idea as far as she was concerned. But Bunty was incapable of logical thought. She droned on about her biological clock and how lovely it would be to buy toys at Christmas, sing carols round the fire, *all three of them*.

Then one evening Zippy came home to find Bunty peering down a microscope.

'Hey, what gives?' said Zippy, nervously. Bunty had been acting strangely for weeks now but here she was, fully present, and her face glowing with a kind of triumph.

'Get yourself over here,' she said. 'This is amazing.'

Zippy stepped back. 'Whoa! Tell me what you're doing first.' Nobody took Zippy for a mug, she remembered the science lessons at school – rub ink around the top of a microscope and ask someone to have a look. Ha bloody ha.

'C'mon,' coaxed Bunty. 'They won't bite. I've just had Cookie deliver a sample for me.' Cookie – the community gofer and Zippy's best friend. She owned a transit van and made a living shifting furniture. Zippy wiped her finger round the top of the barrel and when it came away clean she gingerly lowered her eye and squinted. Illuminated on the slide were hundreds of twitching squiggles.

'Ugh.' She lifted her head. 'I've only just taken that cat to the vet as well.'

Bunty laughed. 'No, you idiot, don't you know what they are? Little tadpole things, with tails . . . ?'

A vague notion of another science lesson drifted into her head.

'Sperms? You've brought a load of sperms into the house?' Zippy stepped back. Her mind racing. Somewhere a man with a red face and sticky hands lurked behind a door. Instinct caused her to reach for a J-cloth. But Bunty merely nodded calmly, arms crossed, looking pleased with herself.

'Cookie knows a bunch of blokes who wank into a jar and she delivers it to ovulating women. What do yer think, Zip, this could be the answer . . .'

Zippy was reeling. She had a vision of Cookie in white

coat and surgical gloves, her pockets bulging with jamjars, answering the call of the ovulating women. It was too much to take in. They'd talked about this baby thing on and off for months, and Zip thought she'd made her feelings plain. She hadn't exactly said 'over my dead body' but to bring a child into the world now – it just wasn't a good time. She had the living room to decorate, a new floor to be laid in the hall. And then there was the VW camper that she was stripping down for a friend.

'Wait a minute,' she said and planted her feet firmly on the floor. She pulled herself up to her full five foot eight-and-a-half inches. 'You're talking about it as though you're ordering a pint of semi-skimmed from the milkman. I mean. You've got to be careful with this stuff.'

Bunty groaned. 'Zip. Don't you think I've thought of that? It's okay – the blokes have been tested.'

'But do you know *anything* about them?'

Bunty twisted her face. 'You're just mad because I've gone ahead and done something on my own for once.'

'What?' bellowed Zippy.

Bunty looked at her full in the face, her jaw set at such an angle you could have hung a coat on it. 'Zip, I'm going ahead with this whether you like it or not.'

Early next morning, before Bunty lifted her pretty little head from the pillow, Zippy was on the blower to Cookie breathing fire into the handset.

'You're supposed to be my best mate,' she hissed.

'So?' Cookie was still sleepy. It was seven o'clock, Saturday morning.

'How come you go and do a thing like that, putting ideas into Bunty's head about sperm donors and stuff...'

'Hang on, Zip...'

'And to give her a bit of spunk to play with...that's gross. Cookie. Really is. You've made everything ten times worse. The whole thing's gone to her head.'

'She really wants this Zippy, you can't keep on ignoring it.'

'Ignoring it? If only. It's me she's ignoring.'

Zippy slammed the phone down. Bunty and her stupid ideas. It was like the time she wanted a dog. Zippy calmly explained that a dog would be impossible. Dogs chew things and Zip was damned if she was going to spend half her life making handcrafted furniture to be destroyed by a smelly Jack Russell. Then Bunty went on about a holiday in Peru. Didn't she realise they'd be robbed and raped before they left the airport? And as for the idea of buying a cream carpet... Come to think of it Bunty was full of stupid notions – but this one took the biscuit.

Pressure cookers, cameras, mopeds, sofas; there wasn't a damn thing in this world that Zippy couldn't fix. Sure she'd never tried her hand to a baby before but she took the challenge on the chin. Everything would be okay, she'd see to it. They'd talked and talked for the best part of four days. Babies, the Relationship, they'd even got on to Names. Bunty had pledged her life that she'd never leave Zippy, but a baby was what she wanted most in the world and she'd do anything to make it happen. Zippy was starting to come round. It was Bunty with baby or no Bunty at all, that much was clear.

And so it began; their monthly pact with the Goddess of Fertility. January, February, March. April, May. No signs of pregnancy but Bunty became obsessed with her nipples. Were they darker, larger, the breasts more veiny? She once thrust her breasts in Zip's face during *Match of the Day*, unforgivable considering it was the cup final. Pregnancy was a fixation with her. Nothing else mattered. Where once Bunty had waxed lyrical about Zip's dovetail joints, now the only thing that brought a gleam to Bunty's eye was the congealing fluid that lay at the bottom of the jar.

Zippy confided in Cookie one day. 'She's just not

interested in me any more. She's got her sights fixed on becoming a family from a cornflakes advert,' she said.

Cookie laughed. 'Eh, listen to you. You're jealous of a dollop of spunk...'

Bunty was acting strangely. She'd taken to going for a walk before bed. Sometimes she was gone for nearly an hour, mostly on foot but sometimes taking the car. Zippy wondered what the hell was going on. One evening, they'd been watching telly for three hours on the trot when Zippy yawned and stretched over to where Bunty lay sprawled across the sofa.

'Coming upstairs?' she asked, but watched incredulously as Bunty reached for her shoes.

'I'm just popping out. I'll be up soon,' said Bunty.

'What?'

'I won't be long.'

'But it's dark.'

'I'll be fine.'

The door slammed behind her.

Plan your work and work your plan. Time to put stage two into action, thought Zippy, as Bunty was getting worse. She'd always been such a gentle soul but these days it was f-ing this and f-ing that and sometimes even Zippy caught the raw end of her tongue. It was the anger she said. It had been fifteen months now since they'd started inseminating and all the creative visualisations and rune stones in the world had drawn an absolute blank. As Bunty became more and more obsessed – focused, she called it – she issued a ban on the sound of scraping, drilling and hammering as she said it upset her equilibrium. Zippy submitted to this maniacal imposition in order to keep the peace as Bunty was liable to fall into a sulk at the drop of a hat. As for sex – it had stopped weeks ago. Bunty dictated that in order to open up her kundalini chakra she needed to keep her legs closed. Zip could live with that for a while, but giving up DIY was akin to having her hands chopped off. She needed a solution quick.

'Stage two,' announced Zippy. 'What we need is fresher, spunkier sperm. We'll meet up with Cookie nearer the donor.'

In a Safeways' carpark on a lonely road, somewhere. Two women in a bashed-up Renault. Zippy looked at her watch for the tenth time wondering what had happened as Cookie was nearly an hour late. If only she'd remembered her mobile.

'C'mon fuck-face. We're going home. I've had enough.' Bunty started the engine and kangarooed out of the carpark.

'Bunty! Calm down, please.'

When they reached home, Bunty stomped upstairs, slamming the door behind her. The phone rang downstairs. It was Cookie.

'Where were you? I've been waiting ages,' she said.

'Christ. Cookie. We've just got in. We've been waiting an hour.'

'Where? I didn't see you.'

'Safeways, of course.'

'Fuck,' Cookie groaned. 'You were meant to come to Asda.'

'You're joking.'

'No. I told you. Asda. I even wrote it down.'

'Oh, fuck.'

'What a waste of time. This stuff is totally dried up. Useless.'

But Zippy had an idea. 'Bring it round anyway.'

'But...'

'Don't argue. Bunty's going ballistic, she's got to have something to put in that syringe.'

'Eh?'

'Please, Cookie. I know what I'm doing.'

It was a stroke of genius inspired by an incident involving a Heinz sponge pudding and a tin of Ambrosia Devon custard. She'd troughed through a whole tin by herself the previous day. It was comfort eating precipitated by yet another row. While washing up she noticed that water added to the pale custard produced a mucusy liquid that resembled semen. In the right light, let's say candlelight, Bunty would never know the difference and Zippy would be let off the hook.

Bunty had been prowling about in the dark outside trying to achieve an elevated mental state, she said, and was now skulking in the bedroom. Zippy felt proud of herself, she loved using her initiative. She felt brighter than she'd done for some time as she tapped gently on the door.

'What the fuck do you want...' said Bunty eventually, opening the door to reveal a tear-stained face.

'It's all right. Situation under control.'

'What do you mean? What happened?'

'Nothing. Cookie made a cock up about the time. She went round the donor's house, he wasn't in. Then she remembered he'd changed the time. She's been outside his house for an hour until he turned up. She's on her way here.'

Bunty stared hard at her. 'Are you sure? She's got the stuff?'

'Trust me, babe, she's bringing it round.'

Stage three. Plan your work and work your plan. It seemed so simple, Zippy wondered why she hadn't thought of it before. Ever since the fateful day when Bunty announced her decision, their lives had been catapulted into a kind of hell. The passing of every month brought tears, rows, smashed plates, disaster. Even Bunty recognised that all was not well. She'd decided to try for just two more months. Two more months of custard semen and all their troubles would be over.

A new life was dawning, their old life resurrected but shining more brilliantly than ever before. There would be parties and gatherings and trips to the Ideal Home Exhibition. There would be design ideas, extensions, transformations and makeovers. Zippy's plans would be back on track and, who knows, within a year or two they could be featured in *Homes and Gardens* – the first lesbian couple to be seen relaxing in a conservatory. The thought of what lay ahead filled Zippy with an irrepressible cheerfulness. It called for a celebration – a little gathering perhaps. It had been ages since they'd invited people round to the house. There would be indoor fireworks, a barbecue, karaoke even. It would be good for Bunty to have something else to think about apart from eggs and urine. It might cheer her up a bit.

Zippy waited for the best time to catch her – post-meditation was usually good.

'I think it would be great if we had a few friends round. For a party. You know, like the old days.'

Bunty shrugged.

'We could really go to town. It might take your mind off things. We could pick a theme. It could be great, Bunt. See all our old mates again.'

Bunty continued to look uninterested.

'You mustn't give up on your friends, Bunt.' Zippy's voice took on a beseeching quality: 'You'll be needing all the support you can get when you're...you know...' she curved her hand over her stomach, 'with child.'

Bunty sat down heavily.

'Well I suppose so. Let me think.'

The sun was shining and the weather was hot. Zippy had a new project to immerse herself in, one that had nothing to do with Babies and she was happy to set to work. They'd decided on a Peter Pan theme so she set about building a replica ship's poop deck after seeing the video. They were to come dressed as their favourite character. Zippy would be Peter and Bunty, Wendy. All their friends would be there. Women they'd not seen for months. Bunty had even relented on the hammering front, justifying the change of heart by saying that the simple sounds of artisan creativity might stimulate her eggs to work. For a solid week, each night after work, Zippy toiled away in the garage, sawing and measuring until their backyard began to take on the appearance of an eighteenth-century tea clipper. First the decking appeared, followed swiftly by the sculpted helm of the ship. The curved sides had been tricky to orchestrate but with a bit of perseverance and help from her new Black and Decker Do-it-all tool she felt she'd made a fine job of them. Cookie dropped round the day before with some frozen vegeburgers.

'So what happened last month?' she asked Zip as they sat in the kitchen.

'What are you on about?'

'About the stuff, what was the deal?'

'Shhh.'

'What?'

'I thought we might as well use it even though it was a little…aged. Just in case there were any still wriggling.'

'It's only potent for an hour, less probably. There's no way Bunt can get pregnant on that.'

'Well you know…'

The appointed day came.

It was 2p.m. and the pirates were starting to arrive. Zippy had never seen so many women with eye patches in one room before. A couple were at the kitchen table – two Captain Hooks having an arm wrestling match to the sound of clashing metal. The barbecue charcoal was hotting up and outside on the patio – the one that Zippy had laid two years ago – a congregation of lost boys were forming around Cookie dressed as Tinkerbell. She was wearing a net curtain and carrying an alarm clock with a very loud tick. 'She doesn't even know the story,' hissed Bunty, who regarded herself as the perfect Wendy with her Victorian pinafore smock bought from an antique shop.

Zippy was in her element as Peter Pan in a slap-my-thigh

jerkin and American Tan tights. She was standing at the barbecue studying the tools: the spear, the fork, the fish tongs, the skewers. All these weapons to bag a few Quorn burgers and veggie sausages. It was a shame, really. Zip wanted to go the whole hog – dripping steaks, breasts of chicken, chops and more chops – but Bunt insisted. Nothing with a face would be cremated at her barbecue she said. What with all the chemicals and food scares, one sniff of a beefburger might be enough to tip her hormone balance right over the edge. Zippy submitted. It was the last indignity. Soon everything would be back to normal.

Pirates, lost boys and someone wrapped in a sheepskin rug answering to the name of Nana stood around, balancing paper plates in one hand, wine glasses in the other, munching, talking. Nobody noticed as a woman in a Victorian pinafore dress, slipped quietly away. There was music, some dancing. The sun burned overhead like a bowl of fire. The first time Zippy realised something was up was when she felt a strong pull on her jerkin. It was Bunty.

'Look!' She shrieked, 'Look at this!!' She waved a plastic stick in Zippy's face. There was a frightening gleam in her eye.

Zippy felt scared. 'What?' She yelped 'What?'

'It's positive.'

Positive?

Zippy saw a blue line on a plastic stick and realised she was looking at a pregnancy test. Bunty screamed and the party burst into a spontaneous roar. 'Wroooooooah,' they shouted. Some spilt their wine and some choked on their burgers and some secretly wished it was happening to them, some wished they'd stayed in to watch *Blind Date* and others didn't really give a damn, but all Zippy could do was stare.

At Bunty.

At Cookie.

And back to Bunty. Slack-jawed and reeking of charcoal, Zippy stared at her friends, the sound of tick tock, tick tock growing louder and louder.

Menaka

Jocelyn Watson

Menaka didn't go to the gym that Monday. She meant to but she was restless and instead popped round to see her friend Amina, who persuaded her to stay for food and some drinks. Menaka thought of telling Amina – telling her everything – especially after the wine, but knew she couldn't. The result of this unexpected dinner was that Menaka arrived home a few minutes late, but there was no message on the answerphone. Menaka immediately phoned Bombay. There was no reply.

Menaka ran her fingers through her short dark hair again and again as she paced up and down the kitchen. Where was Lira? She should be home by now.

Menaka went into the bedroom and looked across at the batik painting of the two Indian women that Lira had given her. It held pride of place on Menaka's wall. Why was there no message? Menaka wanted Lira's presence, Lira's voice.

Just as Menaka reached for the phone again, it rang.

'I tried earlier but you weren't in. Anyway I'm phoning from my friend's place. She's ill so I'm staying with her and can't talk now. I'll call you tomorrow at the same time.'

Menaka replaced the receiver and sighed in exasperation before taking herself to bed. When she awoke next morning her pillows were lying on the floor and her duvet was twisted around her feet. She could feel bags under her usually bright eyes and her caffé-latte skin was taught and grey. She got herself to work but the day dragged and her thoughts drifted.

That Saturday in August. August 2000. A call.

'Hi, Menaka. It's your cousin Lira. Remember me?' a tentative Indian lilting voice had enquired.

'Of course. Lira, how are you? Where are you?'

'I'm in Bombay but I have to go to Paris for a conference at the end of the month and was thinking that as I was so close, it would be good to come to London to see my cousin after all these years.'

'Wonderful.'

'Are you sure?'

'Of course I am. It must be twenty-odd years since we've seen each other. I finish work at about five and I'm usually home by about six. Call me from Paris and let me know when you'll be arriving. Give my love to everyone.'

Menaka didn't chat as she knew that calls from Bombay were expensive. She calculated that in fact it had been nearly thirty years since she had seen Lira. Menaka had been in her early teens when Lira had arrived in Newcastle with her Bangalorean husband and young baby. Menaka remembered her cousin making her laugh a lot and recalled going shopping with Lira and baby Anita, but had no other recollections except that she had gotten on well with Lira and they had liked each other. Menaka knew that Lira worked as a psychologist, and painted in her spare time. On many occasions over the years, various relatives had told Menaka that she and Lira should meet.

Menaka returned home that Thursday, stopping at her local butcher to purchase Cumberland sausages and two pieces of fresh free-range organic chicken. Just as she was considering whether to deal with the dust and the papers that also occupied her flat, the telephone rang.

'Hi Menaka, it's Lira.'

'Where are you?'

'I'm in Chinatown and I've been having a great time going to the places I used to hang out, in my student days.'

'Haven't they been demolished by now?'

'What a cheek. I'm not that much older than you.'

'Twenty years.'

'Array?'

'Only kidding. Tell the driver you want to go to Tottenham off Philip Lane. It should take you about an hour.'

Menaka put the phone down and started on the chicken breasts, marinating them in sesame oil, soya sauce, chilli sauce and garlic. There was fresh spinach in the fridge, which she washed and chopped, and basmati rice, which she soaked. She set the table, lit some candles and then proceeded to roll a joint while she listened to Me'Shell Ndegeocello. Halfway through the joint, the doorbell sounded and Menaka rushed down the stairs. She opened the door to the welcoming arms of a short Indian woman, more or less the same height as herself with long dark hair that ended at her breasts. From her ears dangled a panoply of colour, which was echoed in the flair of her mulmul cotton dress. Lira looked as young as she had done thirty years ago. Her skin was a roasted coffee bean brown and unblemished. Her cheekbones were high and below her arched eyebrows, her peacock eyes were luring. Menaka immediately remembered her cousin for the smile that she had not lost.

'I can't believe we finally meet again after all these years.'

'Yes, isn't it fantastic.'

As they both struggled up the stairs with all the luggage, Lira noticed that Menaka's eyes were focused on her feet.

'I just don't wear shoes in the house,' Menaka interjected.

'Why didn't you tell me before?'

'I'm not that precious about it. I just find it cathartic. Leave your worries at the door.'

'Just like home,' Lira patted Menaka's leg.

Menaka retrieved a pair of chappals and gave them to Lira.

'Take my worries away,' Lira demanded, exchanging her Indian sandals for Menaka's chappals. 'So you and I have the same size feet. I hope that's not all we have in common.' Lira opened her eyes wide and stared at Menaka.

'We've got a week to find out. Are you hungry? What about a drink?'

'I'm not a great drinker but I thought the occasion warranted something special and no better place to buy it from than France, so here you are,' said Lira, retrieving a bottle of Moët et Chandon champagne from her suitcase and handing it to Menaka.

'Lira, thank you. Oh dear, a cousin with expensive taste. I don't know if I'll be able to keep up with the Mascarenhases,' Menaka responded, adding, 'I'll just go chill this in the freezer, shall I?'

Returning to the living room, she found Lira waiting with a red-wrapped package. 'And I brought this, especially for you.'

Smiling with anticipation, Menaka carefully began to unwrap the gift – a folded batik full of colours from home.

'Oh, this is wonderful. It's Goa isn't it?'

Lira nodded, adding, 'I painted it twenty years ago but I thought it . . . it might be just right for you.'

'Lira, it's fabulous.'

Menaka spread the batik over the sofa. On background colours of cobalt blue and burnt sienna, one woman was lying on the beach at Vagator, with only her pink choli and pink petticoat on, while the other woman, dressed in a red and yellow sari looked down at her, with a smile.

'Oh, thank you. I love it.'

'I thought you might. I've heard all the family rumours that you've turned your back on your . . . middle-class Goan Catholic heritage but your flat looks great – not the improvised hovel I expected from a socialist.'

'Oh, no. Don't you start. You've only just got through

the door. You're supposed to be civil and polite at least for a day.'

Lira laughed. 'Forget it. You're family and I get to say exactly what I like.' She flippantly ruffled Menaka's hair and pinched her arm. 'Or is the English half of you going to get all formal and polite, in which case I'd better not stay long.' Lira's eyebrows rose and the luring smile turned sober for a second.

'Come, let's sit out on the balcony. It's so rare to have such glorious sun-drenched evenings here and I want to hear all your news.' Menaka opened her arms and put one around Lira's shoulders, directing her through the kitchen to the deckchairs on the balcony.

'Wonderful. I'm so glad I thought of ringing you, though I did have my doubts.'

'I'm not that much of an ogre for goodness sake.'

'I know.' Lira shrugged her shoulders, continuing, 'It's just we haven't met in such a long time.'

Menaka went back into the kitchen and emptied a bag of pakoras from Ambala's onto a plate and passed them to Lira and then took the champagne, two glasses and returned to the balcony.

'The last time I saw you, you were a quiet young teenager.'

'You were a married woman with a husband and baby in tow. I just remember going shopping with you and Anita whom you were still breast-feeding and you treating me to a Wimpy.'

Both their faces twisted in disgust.

'I don't really remember that visit except that even though we had barely been married a year and a half, Vikram and I were already arguing. That's probably why it was just you and I out shopping.'

'I heard that you were divorced. It's quite some time ago now.'

'Thirteen years ago, but years too late.'

'How are you enjoying life as a single woman? By the

way, nothing'll be repeated to anyone. Unlike most of the Fonsecas I can keep confidences.'

'Yes, I have heard that you're very diplomatic.' Lira hesitated for a moment. 'I suppose I have the best of both worlds in that I live my life as a single woman but I've been having an affair with a married man that no one knows about.' Lira looked questioningly across at Menaka and directly into her eyes.

Menaka's green-blue eyes and dimples stared back warm and defiant. She leaned across and stroked Lira on the arm.

'How are your mum and Anita?'

'They're fine and send their love. Anita is doing postgraduate work. She has a boyfriend and they've been together since their days at St Xavier's. I'm sure it won't be long before they're married.'

'How sad,' Menaka remarked without thinking who she was talking to.

'Why do you say that?'

'Oh dear, maybe I shouldn't've opened my mouth.'

'I thought you said that it was safe to say anything in this house.'

'It is but it's just that I'm not sure you're going to like what I have to say.'

'Say it. I don't want us to start off thinking that we can't say things to each other because we are frightened what the other'll think.'

'To be perfectly honest...'

'Forget all this English nonsense and just tell me what you think I can't handle hearing.'

'Okay, I don't believe in marriage. I think it's an institution that was set up by men for men. I don't believe that marriage can be anything but oppressive for women.'

Lira looked at Menaka. Lines appeared over her brow and her pupils dilated and her eyes became serious and stern. Lira knew why Menaka didn't believe in marriage but that was her business.

'Well, anyway, it's Anita's decision and she's not here now so you can get off your soapbox. As long as she's happy I really don't care.'

'And your mum, how's she?'

'What to say. She enjoys life in Bombay even if she has a very predictable routine. And you? Tell me about your life. What have you been doing all these years?'

'I'm sure you've heard enough to have some inkling what I've been doing.'

'Yes I think you've provided the family across the globe with a fair amount of gossip.'

'Isn't it astounding, Lira, to think that our great-great-grandparents came from a tiny fishing village in Goa and now we're to be found on all five Continents with a grapevine that's faster than the Internet.'

'The accuracy of that leaves a lot to be desired.'

They both laughed in recognition and went on to talk about their fifty-odd cousins, their aunts and uncles and other members of their extended family for hours till Menaka, realising that it was late, shuffled Lira indoors while she prepared the dinner.

'What would you like to do in the week you're here?'

'I want to visit galleries, go to the theatre, and to any other places that have sprung up while I've been away.'

Over dinner they meticulously planned Lira's week. Phone calls from Lira and Menaka's other relatives in England interrupted their meal. Menaka's mother wanted Lira and Menaka to visit her in Leeds, which they tactfully declined. At half two Menaka finally made suggestions about sleep.

'Your options are either to share my bed or this sofa converts into a bed, so whichever you feel happiest with,' Menaka said, looking at Lira with no idea how she would reply.

'Important question, do you snore?'

'No. Do you?'

'Good. Well in that case, I'd be happy to share a bed with my cousin.'

Menaka gave Lira a white khadi cotton kurta. Lira was completely exhausted from her travels and Menaka from the anticipation of Lira's arrival and the spliffs she'd enjoyed while they'd talked.

The next morning, over breakfast, they decided for Lira's first day, they would go to the Courtauld and then have dim sum, with a leisurely amble through Covent Garden shopping to walk off lunch, before catching a boat down the Thames as respite for their feet. Dinner would be fish and chips wrapped in newspaper for old times' sake, which they'd eat on the Embankment before going to the Cottlesloe to see *The Waiting Room*.

Menaka led them both, ducking and diving through the throngs of tourists, Londoners, students, workers and the homeless whom Lira was astounded to see in such numbers. They were a reminder of home that Lira hadn't expected in the heart of London. Lira slid her hand easily into Menaka's as they rushed for a bus, to catch the Tube or even as they walked down the South Bank.

Shabana Azmi, the Indian star in Tanika Gupta's *The Waiting Room*, was Menaka and Lira's favourite actress.

'Have you seen her in *Fire*?' enquired Menaka, feeling more confident to speak frankly to Lira.

'No, not yet. The trouble bloody Shiv Sena have caused about the film, because of its content, is ridiculous,' Lira casually commented as she looked through Menaka's bookshelves.

'Its lesbian content, you mean?' Menaka asked emphatically.

'Yes,' Lira replied, aware that Menaka was watching her closely. 'I would like to see it.'

'We'll get the video out from the local library if you'd like.'

'Perhaps we could come home earlier tomorrow. Today's been busy. I've enjoyed myself but perhaps it was just a bit too much. It would be good to come back and just relax. We could watch it then and I could cook us a meal.'

They collapsed into bed and sleep.

The next day Lira made fresh parathas for breakfast to go with the Cumberland sausages.

'Did you ever have Nana's parathas in Bombay when you were a kid?'

'Yes. Whenever we visited from England, she'd sit with me on the balcony and watch as I ate, encouraging me to eat more.'

'She'd do the same with us too. We were lucky we got to see Nana every summer holiday. Anyway, I'm certainly not as good a cook as Nana but I've made a list so take me to your local Indian store.'

'Sure, but I thought you might like to go for a leisurely walk to Hampstead Heath to the Women's Pond. I thought we could have a picnic there and perhaps shop on our return.'

'What's the Women's Pond? No men I guess?' Lira disapprovingly suggested.

'No men indeed and some of the women are nunga punga.'

'No, thank you. Number one, I'm not one of those women who goes around nunga punga; secondly, I won't swim in this country, you must be mad. You want to do your lesbian thing, you have to count me out, Menaka.'

So they went to St Ann's Library and the Indian Food Hall and returned home early. While Menaka set up the video, Lira began to prepare their meal. They watched *Fire* and over dinner discussed the political impact the film had had in Bombay. They feasted on seekh kebab, sag paneer, kuchumbar, raita and chicken biryani, finishing with rasmalai before agreeing to go to bed.

As they both lay in bed, Lira asked Menaka if she'd like a massage. 'My speciality. Not that I make that common knowledge.'

'That'd be wonderful.'

'Do you have any cream?'

'I've got some Body Shop Vitamin E cream.'

'That'll do. Not as good as coconut oil or Vicco Ayurvedic haldi skin cream,' remarked Lira with dissatisfaction.

Menaka went to the bathroom, returned with the cream and took off the red cotton nightdress she was wearing. She lay on the bed face down and Lira climbed over her and knelt with a leg either side of Menaka's waist. She poured cream over Menaka's back.

'Array your skin is smooth.'

'Do you think so?'

'It feels as soft as a baby feels.'

Menaka let herself be pampered by the skilful movements of Lira's fingers. No one had stroked her body in a long time. Menaka had last felt the gentleness of another human being's touch six years previously with her former lover, Shani, and since then she had been on her own.

'Okay turn over,' Lira ordered.

Menaka turned. Lira seemed unperturbed by Menaka's nakedness and so Menaka basked in the relaxation of Lira's fingers gliding around her neck, her breasts, her arms, her stomach and down her legs. Menaka opened her eyes and looked directly at Lira. Lira smiled.

'Does this feel good?'

'It feels wonderful.' Menaka stretched out her arms to Lira's and used them to pull herself up.

When Menaka's face was up close to Lira's, she delicately touched Lira's lips with her fingers and then with her own lips. Menaka did it again and Lira's lips welcomed Menaka's and their tongues met for an instant and then again and again. Both their mouths opened to each other and their tongues explored and moved around each other's mouths.

Newness gave way to passion, intense and feverish. As their tongues moved their hands followed suit over each other's bodies with tenderness and affection. They rolled into each other, constantly caressing each other and whispering each other's names. Their bodies trembled and quivered with excitement. They acknowledged physically as well as verbally the pleasure that each enjoyed from and with the other. They held each other tight and eventually sleep enveloped them.

In the morning they awoke in each other's arms and for the last three days of Lira's visit they remained together at home. They made love again and again knowing that it would be a long time before they would see each other after Lira left. They went out only to get milk and fresh-baked bread from the Italian deli. Menaka took the phone off the hook and they permitted no one to interrupt the unadulterated ecstasy they were experiencing.

On the last morning they were both silent. Menaka helped Lira to pack and they ordered a taxi to Heathrow. They sat in the back seat; Menaka allowed her dupatta to fall over Lira's hand so that their fingers could touch, out of the taxi driver's view. At the departure gate they held tight to each other for a moment and kissed each other on the cheek as cousins, as Lira had made Menaka promise at home. There was to be no public exhibition of their love and Lira would not countenance going to the women's toilet, which would have been the only place where they might have one last passionate embrace.

'I'll call you on Monday evening about nine-thirty your time, after you get back from the gym and speak to you then. Take care of yourself, Menaka. I had a lovely time with you and I'm so glad that we have met again at last.'

'I love you, Lira,' Menaka whispered as Lira stroked Menaka's right hand.

Nodding, Lira replied quietly, 'And I, you,' before she walked off through the departure gates and disappeared.

The phone rang. Menaka knew it was Lira. She hesitated and then answered.

'Hello, Menaka. It's Lira.'

'Hi. So you're home. You must be exhausted.'

'I am. I am because this last week with you in London has turned me upside down. Menaka, you're a lovely woman. You and I have so much in common, so much to share and we are…we are so alike. You are everything that I've always wanted in a lover. We are kindred spirits but Menaka but I'm not like you. I can't face the world with pride as you do. I don't want to be a lesbian. I want to be normal. I want to be heterosexual. This is too daunting. I'm not brave enough to take this on.' The sentences burst out of Lira's mouth as though her throat were being throttled.

'What are you talking about? I don't care about labels, Lira. I saw and felt what you felt. I was with you and you showed me and told me you loved me.'

'That was then. Now I know better. Now I'm home in Bombay. I know who I am and what I am.'

'What's happened?'

'I saw Raj. I know now that I'm not a lesbian like you.'

'Are you telling me that you left me and went back and had sex with Raj?'

'Yes, Menaka. I'm sorry. But I'm heterosexual. I know now that's what I am.'

'What about what you felt with me?'

'It happened. It was beautiful. I want you, but I can't. What can I say?'

'More than you're saying now, Lira. For Christ's sake Lira, we were locked in each other's arms, in each other's love for three intense days. What do you want from love?'

'I'm sorry, Menaka. I don't want to be a lesbian. Not at this stage of my life. I have friends here who would never understand. What about Anita? I have the only life that I'll ever have here at home in Bombay.'

'Why, Lira? Why? We can face the world together and anyway what do other people's prejudice and narrow-mindedness matter? We can meet up, we can write to each other and talk to each other. The technology now exists for us to communicate whenever we want. We have found something special, Lira. We can be there for each other.'

'We are cousins, Menaka. We will always be there for each other.'

'Lira, stop it. We're lovers. We can't pretend that nothing happened.'

'Nobody must ever know. Menaka promise me you will never tell anyone, ever. No one in the family must ever find out.'

'I promise. I promise,' Menaka was choking with pain, as she assured Lira. 'I told you, when you were here that I won't tell anyone and I meant it. Lira, listen to me. We did nothing wrong. We met. We fell in love. We realised how well we get on intellectually, emotionally, oh, everything, physically, sexually. We fell in love. We did nothing wrong. We have nothing to be ashamed of. We could have a wonderful relationship. We could grow from strength to strength. You are what I want. You are everything I desire and love.'

'Menaka, I'm sorry for the pain I have caused you. I don't want to talk about this ever again. It happened. It was a sin. Nothing like this will ever happen again between us, Menaka. I have to go now. Forgive me.'

Honey Says
Sophie Levy

It's Easter Sunday, about 8 a.m. Christ and I have both risen, but while he is out catching up with old friends and making new enemies, I am sitting in the kitchen, rubbing the arch of my foot against the blonde curve of the table leg. Thinking of you. My fingers shape scattered crumbs into hillocks, like a child building sandcastles, but the activity is only an excuse. The table seemed so raw when I bought it, bleeding sap when I stuck it with the bread knife; now butter-soft. Time and things change.

I trace the scar with a fingernail, worrying at it as if it were part of my own skin. One side of it is the gold of sponge cake, the other fallen into shadow. The sunlight gets everywhere in the kitchen, even into the puttied cracks between the tiles, and around each grape in the fruit bowl. It slides across the stark, white plyboard work surfaces, powers the buzz of the fridge, the burn of the toaster. I jump to catch a muffin, tanned by this, the first real spring day of the year. The toasted scent is solid and transparent, a prism, refracting the light of the morning into smell.

The knife leaves buttery lumps in the new jar of honey, and I remove them with a guilty finger until I remember that it is my honey, my lumps. I am still thinking of you secretively as I make tea, with supermarket tea bags and yesterday's milk. The hot water is licking into the cup you used the first time you ever sat in this kitchen. Steam, rising off the cold milk into the chill dawn, makes the world timeless.

'We discussed desire,' you said, 'at 3 a.m.' Your voice at the other end of the line. What was there before nothingness. The paradox of a presence without substance. I concur with a 'Hmm,' and continue to dry between my toes. As the silence expands, I feel I must justify myself, my silence, my words.

'I was pissed, wasn't I?'

'Hammered.' I laugh shallowly as you describe me, tripping over your white rug as we entered your flat, waving my arms in expansive gestures of greeting. 'You were only about half-there, if you know what I mean.'

'See,' I exclaim triumphantly, as if you have solved your problem, proved my point. 'It was the forgetful half that was there,' I lie, remembering all this clearly with a shame that spreads into my cheeks like (what else?) a wine stain. 'Sorry about the carpet,' I volunteer hesitantly, 'but I don't remember much else.' The apology is intended for the forgetting as well as the stain. I leave the bathroom because the heat has evaporated while we have paused and been unsure.

The silence at your end has grown cold, too. As I am pulling on a dressing gown and secreting my feet under the bedcovers, I hear you mumbling petulantly. 'Sorry, I...I can't hear you,' I say, and you sigh and repeat your words, slower, louder.

'Don't worry about the carpet. I thought you might...' You stop, as if there are no words in my vocabulary you could use to explain what we said and did. You sound as if I had betrayed you by forgetting. I own up haltingly, unwilling to allow the false silence to continue or an argument to develop. I remember every word I said in the candlelit half-dark of your bedroom, but I cannot tell you this. You are right. The words are absent from me, in the not-there of you.

So I say,

'Whatever I said . . .' I pause, shy, my face and stomach flushed with tiredness and desire, 'whatever, I was drunk.' Implication – you got me drunk. 'I don't say half of what I mean when I'm sober, and I don't mean half of what I say when I'm pissed.' A beautiful parallel, Wildean you would later inform me, an excuse and a lie. Please try to read between the lines, I meant, please understand that I want this but do not know the words to ask. I can hear in your silence that you are one step ahead of me, patient but growing less so. 'Why don't you come over here? We can discuss whatever again. Sober.'

'No,' you said, wounded still, giving in to the irrational. 'I'll see you around.' There was a forlorn tone to your voice. Two people who met by accident do not 'see each other around'.

The phone signal clicked out, possibility shutting down like a book. I left the phone receiver in a puddle of condensation that has formed on the window ledge, spinning and impotent. I pulled the covers up over my knees and rested my forehead on the bridge of my forearms. Who have I betrayed? So I had forgotten, or intimated that I had forgotten, what in fact I remembered, tearful, pre-dawn confessions that tasted of acrid cigarette smoke and unbrushed teeth. They had no meaning, those seeping phrases tinged with fear and the green of 3 a.m. The betrayal started there, in the nowhere made more so by my lie.

'We discussed desire,' you said, 'at 3 a.m.' Here you are in my kitchen; here we are, face to face in the sullen light of November 4 p.m. I offer you a coffee as I anticipate your detection of my lie. There are no chances to hide, not even in the deep blue stains that twilight slips across the sky, and the blue-grey bruises welling up on the skin of the kitchen. The year has become too old for deception, and judges me harshly. I smile at you weakly, and watch the eddies in my greying tea. The overcast, rainy glow is merciless, giving me no bright diversion. Monotone and melancholy, it grubs you and I and the kitchen and the world in the same shade of over-washed white. The grey of the light gets into my eyes like grit.

You watch me as I use up pastel tissues. Your words are still in the room, resonating against the cupboards and the floor, the television screen and the breadboard. They all remain blank, silent, embarrassed by this confession. I have no answer for them. All that November allows is truth. We discussed desire at 3 a.m. We talked about lust in the green-black hour of the goblin, of the heart attack, the prank call and the end of arguments.

'We discussed desire,' you said gently, 'at 3 a.m.' You smiled at me. The smile, the discussion. The stain of them spread like sweet butter over us, over the late nights and breakfasts of three honeyed years.

I have no need to remember more, to have these memories rising like clouds of steam off the cold milk in the bottom of my cup as the steaming water splashes in, splashes me. Tiny pinpricks of unbearable heat, like desire; there are clusters of small heat blisters on my hands and a flush steaming up my cheeks. I am craving sweetness, I am biting into the sticky gold layer of syrup on a cinnamon Danish.

There was a time when I never ate, when food shone plastic and dizzied me with the brightness of the light it reflected. I could not eat, could not persuade myself that under the plastic shell of illusion was nourishment. A Danish was a coiled loop of intestines writhing under a gleam of blood and bile. Now I bite into the jellied blobs of syrup to grab hold of life. I push my teeth through the spicy layers of pastry that start off brown and crisp, flaking away. Autumn leaves. Old paint on park benches where we used to sit and argue.

I used to pick at the flaking paint until I revealed the dull metal beneath, until your harangue had finished and I could walk off towards the pale blue sky left behind by the rising sun. The grass fell beneath my boots with an eerie breaking sound, glassy with frost, and the leaves lay impaled on it, rotting. The sharp taste of cinnamon is like breathing in that wintry air, swallowing arctic chills to stop the tears that you could always charm from my eyes, make dance down my cheeks.

Under the flaky, sad brown there are layers of doughy pastry that stick slightly to my teeth but melt away on my tongue. A taste of scrambling into a wide hotel bed in a wild afternoon, tearing back the stiff brown coverlet, and sliding under a dozen different creamy layers. Your laughter is in my ears as I disappear below endless billows of sheets. Lick the small cinnamon freckles on your pale skin. They do not dissolve to a memory of spice.

Still, in the morning, there we are, eating feverishly in the pastry bed, twined in the cheap cotton sheets, laughing and moaning to drown out the mundane buzz of the vacuum cleaner outside the door. The pastry layers of my Danish are resilient, pliant, like your skin under my inexperienced mouth. There are sudden pockets of dark, smooth fruit syrup. It tastes of summer sweat soaking into sheets and pillowcases. I only notice the weight of my own body when I lost the soft burden of a lover. I have begun to eat as if I could make myself two.

There is none of the heaviness of that summer here in the bright spring kitchen. Outside the birch trees throw a silver patina over the grass. I swallow the last bite of Danish, draw breath too suddenly. A childish breeze teases the petals of the snowdrops and the delicate bluebells. The daffodils, far more sturdy, barely sway their splendid golden heads. Last year we found a double-headed one and kept it on the desk in the bedroom for weeks, until it dried and we found its shrivelled petals crumbled in our books. The metaphor turned cliché.

The stems I cut yesterday are still seeping clear, greenish

sap into the vase. It swirls in the water, leaving a viscous pattern like the whorls of syrup left on my fingers. I am picking up crumbs from the table with the tip of an adhesive finger. The crumbs are gritty on my tongue, mixed with dirt from the table surface. I feel dirty eating them. There's not even crumbs left of you here, no blonde hairs in my hairbrush, no peach-fuzz dust of face powder on my porcelain sink, not even an old photograph of you, smiling your askew smile and looking away from the camera at me. In the photograph, I would have disappeared into the blurred red patch that bleeds out from the right-hand side as if something had spilt on the lens.

The non-existent photograph stops my breath as if time had not progressed from the moment it wasn't taken. My desire to hold my breath until – to earn the kiss of life from you. Breathe. Don't think. 'Don't create,' you would say. Time changes. Breathe.

But that breath touches the empty place of pain above my lungs. I breathe again, to feel that corrosive ache. It makes my spine loose and the part of my brain that stores memories swells and throbs. You told me where it was once, drawing invisible equators on my skull with the edge of your thumbnail. I suck in breath again, letting it spiral deeper and deeper into the wound. Always eager to fall victim to your off-handed cruelties, your petty harm.

Memory floats up, glides up like a marsh wraith. It is as dangerous and elusive as the hobgoblin, who fires up the gas on the stove and ties your bootlaces together. I can hear you reading these stories to me, footnotes to a programme you are editing for *Peer Gynt*. It was a damp winter, its outlines blurry with drizzle and mist. We laughed together at the stories but, waking at 2 a.m. to find your hollow beside me, I slipped out of bed and stood shadowed in the doorframe, watching you.

I hold that picture of you, creeping downstairs with your hair unravelling from its plait, tight like a Christmas hazelnut inside its shell. You tread softly, careful not to wake me nor to warn the goblins. There are stray hairs caught by static on your cheeks. Although it is winter, you sleep only in boxer shorts. They are children's, thin blue cotton with Mickey Mouse printed over and over on them, but you are wearing them inside out and I can only see the shape of Mickey Mouse where the print has puckered the cotton surface. Your skin is soaking up the darkness as you turn down the stairwell, out of the moonlight and out of my vision. And in the morning there was a length of mistletoe over the doorframe, and the knives were uncrossed in the cutlery drawer.

I hold you inside me; dark, spicy memories of you. I am quartering an apple, and using the quarters to wipe up the pools of honey on the plate. The green skin is bland under its coat of wax, but the white flesh is sharp, bewildering. It slices through the cloy of the honey, parches my throat. It is the wrong time of year for this. I am biting the harvest's bounty six months too early or too late. In September, it didn't occur to me to show you this tradition. You asked me about my religion and I answered with recipes. This is a recipe and a prayer, a custom of autumn, a prayer for sweetness and plenty.

Had we spoken, I could have told you:

'Now, in mid-September, it is the time of change. Rosh Hashanah, the Jewish New Year. It is a time of promise and renewal, start of the Holy Days, the closing of the book on last year.' It is a time when we are weighed by a god blinded by his own cruel sense of justice. We beg forgiveness, abject ourselves before his might. We cast out our sins as crumbs on moving water. We cast out our sinners. All this happens secretly, hidden in our hearts under the waxy veneer of tradition. Poison in the seeds of an apple. Had we spoken, I could have quartered an apple like this, and dipped the point into a dish of honey.

I could have licked the sweetness from your fingers and

tasted the bits of apple left between your crooked teeth. The whole house would be fragrant with the scent of baked apples; cinnamon clouds would sidle out of the oven and through the hall as we tumbled up the stairs, intoxicated on plummy dessert wine and painful memories we'd laughed at together. I would have told you, later, cupping, licking, savouring your apple-like breast:

'The apple is wholeness, round like the world. Promise of fertility and bounty. Its sweetness is the sweetness of doing right.' Its tartness shows us the secret pleasure of biting down on pain. We practise purity, fasting until we burn.

'The honey is bounty, flowing. It also means sweetness, the sweetness of being whole.'

Your breast with its dark nipple-seed rests in my hand like a still life. The memory of you rests in the cusp of my thoughts, in the curve of the spring morning. There is pleasure in the pain of missing you, of biting into the memory of your breast, the memory of biting into your breast. Memories are biting into me, like a pack of wolves at my heels.

'But at my back I always hear
Time's wingèd chariot hurrying near.'

Time doesn't change much. The old poets had it down. You told me that poem was a seduction attempt, lust dressed up as metaphysics. You read me others, teasing me about my earlier passionate defences of my confused sexuality, reminding me of your superior wit, logic and desire.

You read me 'To Virgins, to make much of time', and laughed with mild scorn when I said I had heard it in a film, and you read me John Donne and Horace, all pleading with girlfriends whose morals stood between love and eternity. The message was always the same: '*Carpe diem*'. So I seized you, but you rolled out of bed and sat nude at my desk, translating Horace into English for me, writing out your own version with my cracked-nibbed fountain pen that blotched the paper and stained your fingers. For days, when you talked to me, I would follow your blue fingertips, fascinated. They lay strangely on the sand-coloured couch as we watched old movies, like blue worms waiting to attack you. You even made love to me with those ink-blue, Caliban fingers, as if they could whisper to me the secrets of learning you poured through the pen, the secrets of seduction. Time doesn't change much. Not even desire.

I am learning now about other seductions. There is seduction in silence, too. There is a rising murmur of seduction in loss and mourning, a sensual pleasure you could never understand. Even though it is Passover, dour holiday of unleavened bread and night-long vigils of psalms and prayers, even though my Judaism had trouble outlasting my juvenile crush on the Hebrew schoolteacher, even though you are gone and cannot hear the words, I am slicing up this apple to show you the ritual I never thought meant a thing.

I start by unscrewing the jar lid slowly, a nearly new jar, perfect for Rosh Hashanah, which demands new clothes, new fruit, a new moon. I pour a little honey onto a white china dish, watching, dazed, as the sunlight dapples the pocked, coppery surface of the honey. I wish now I had the words for the ceremony. I wish – briefly – that I had listened to my father reading them, blessing us in his oleaginous voice. I wish that I could run upstairs, my bare toes splaying on each step, and pluck the right book. You always had the right book. I would whisper to you to come down, shake you gently, knowing that you had been awake for hours and luxuriating in the near-sleep somnolence of a Sunday morning. I would smile at your uncomprehending eyes, and kiss the crusts from their corners, then drag you naked down to the kitchen as you yawned and tripped over your sleeping feet.

I would say:

'Here. Eat this wholeness, sweetness.' The metaphor is true. Eat, be part of my ritual.

Then I would open the heavy, ornate volume, and read out the words in my rusty Hebrew as you stood there holding an apple quarter that dripped honey down your arm like the sunlight dripped on the golden down on your belly and legs. I would ask God, some god, any god, even one of your terrifying Norse gods, to bless this mellow, wrong-time-of-year dawn, as you bit into the apple and its ripe, tangy smell filled the kitchen like a golden light.

I wish I had the words; I want to be able reel them up from the deep pool of memory as you did, tossing me your catch: lines of poetry, song lyrics, dialogue from plays and films, quips and quotations from the famous, dictionary definitions. But I have only the hollow where words should be, where you are, the hollow in my bed. I cannot hope to curl up in a space in your mind; you lie full length in mine, dreaming in the empty place left for pain. I have no words for what this ritual really means, for its harvest wholeness and its righteous sweetness, I have only words that I offer you, puddled, swirled, thick but clear.

I say to you:

'Here, eat the apple of wholeness, of us and the beauty of your breast. It is cut into quarters to show how you have splintered me by your beauty and its absence. Each quarter is dipped into honey, as clear and dark as the night you left, glittering with sharp sugar-crystal stars. The honey's sweetness will leave a burnt aftertaste, the aftermath of pleasure. Loss. The dark, liquescent place of pain beneath my heart, the sweet, bitter ache of you gone. The taste which is the memory of taste.' Eat, partake of the ritual.

Partake of the blessing of the spring gods. I sink my teeth into your tart perfection. Come back to me. You words I cannot remember, words I have forgotten to remember for so long. Help me, I am trying to remember sweetness, to find pleasure. I wish I had taken the time. Kept it, glass jarred. Preserved. What this taste reminds me of. Something jarring, deep within pain, within the well of pain in my chest, eating clear, golden honey in the sunshine. Those things of 3 a.m. Crossed knives cut into us. Memories that breathe truth in us, however we lie.

Still Life With Cat
Rhiannon Satis

I painted this kitchen a month before you left. Yellow walls and magnolia woodwork. You laughed and accused me of lacking imagination.

The magpies are busy in the rowan tree at the bottom of the garden. Pecking at the bright red berries. You always loved bright colours. When I first saw you, you were wearing scarlet. I push back a strand of hair, steal a piece of celery from the salad bowl. The garlic I have just chopped adheres to my fingers and the two tastes mingle together in my mouth. I am cooking dinner for friends.

I open the drawer for the tablecloth – catch the scent of lavender. You planted two bushes outside the back door the day you moved in and I use it as my grandmother did – a few sprigs in the drawer to keep the linen smelling sweet. When I go outside to scatter stale bread on the bird table the bees are busy in your lavender bushes. Roving over them like tourists going round a stately home. Marjorie eyes the bird table expectantly. I chide her and she looks at me from slanting green eyes, feigning innocence. In old age she is becoming the matriarch of tabby cats. Full of feline grace and wisdom; but still very capable of hatching plots around my bird table.

The sound of a train carries on the still evening air. It will be bringing my friends from London. I go back into the house, remembering when you met me off the train on an evening exactly like this a year ago. How good it was to breathe the clear air after a day in the city. The tarmac of the station forecourt pleasantly warm under my toes as I slipped off my sandals and we walked to the car. (Bohemian, you used to call me, for my habit of going barefoot all summer.) And all I was thinking of was giving you the silly present I had bought in Oxford Street. A red and yellow parrot on a string. 'Hang it in the kitchen,' I was going to say, 'to make up for my unimaginative colour scheme.' Then we got in the car, I leaned over to kiss you – and you turned your face away and told me you were leaving.

I put the salad in the fridge, take scissors from a drawer and go out to cut flowers for the table. Love-in-a-mist and what will probably be the last roses for this year. I will not ask my friends – have they seen you? Did you ask about me? I decide this as I cut a deep crimson rose with a yellow heart and mark it for the centre of the arrangement. I will not mention your name tonight. A magpie scolds loudly, splitting the evening silence, making me jump. I look up and see him on the topmost branch of the rowan tree, his plumage glossy in the evening sun, notice my finger has been scratched by a thorn. I suck the blood as I walk back to the house. I will not talk about you though I love you and still miss you. But I want this evening to go well and tomorrow morning wake up thick-tongued, hung over. I want to know we all drank a little too much and talked all night. Like in our student days. I have stopped looking for a letter from you each morning. Now I want an evening when I do not think about you.

I arrange the flowers in my mother's crystal vase then open the wine because Marcus will insist it's been left to breathe. A self-confessed wine snob, Jancis Robinson is his guru and goddess. I love the familiarity of my friends. Caro will be bound to enthuse over some new gadget I cannot possibly live without and Stevie, ever the minimalist, urge me not to have it. Familiar, yes, but never predictable, they are more than capable of surprising me. Even after all this time.

As I finish laying the table, I remember how we met. We were at university in the late seventies. I knew Marcus as a face in a lecture hall. But it was Caro I met first. In the loo, of all places. She was desperate for change for the Tampax machine. Stevie was her lover then. We rented a house together and Marcus moved in after we advertised for a fourth person to join us. He spent six months denying he was gay. Then he fell in love with a man who came to fix the plumbing and, at an end-of-term party, came out spectacularly in five yards of tulle and a tiara.

There is still fifteen minutes before they arrive. I turn down the gas under a pan of boiling water – too soon to put the pasta on – pour myself a glass of wine then put Rachmaninov on the CD player and sit down in my favourite chair; the one that overlooks the front garden. Marjorie jumps into my lap and settles to some serious paw washing. The music rises to an orgiastic crescendo. And I can still see us sitting here that evening over our final chess game. (God! How civilised we were.) You seeming intent on the game, and me, wondering – when did you decide this? When we last made love – did you know then? When we planned to go Russia this year – did you know you would not be going with me? The surprise party I organised for your birthday, when you seemed so happy – then? How much of the last eighteen months had been a lie? When you told me you were leaving, you said you couldn't live 'my kind of life'. I watched your hand hover over the chessboard with uncharacteristic hesitation. (I was black, you were white.) And I know my question seemed sarcastic; I was only trying to draw you out. 'So, what is "my kind of life"?' You changed your mind about the bishop, moved your queen to a safer position – and told me you were going back to your husband. I didn't even know you had been in touch with him.

And the following morning – the sound of the hall door closing. How the silence settled around me so that suddenly it was like living in a vast cavern. Not knowing if you could find your way out – if there was a way out. I barely registered the slam of the taxi door, the sound of it driving away.

I have become accustomed to solitude again. Just me and Marjorie.

My hand absently strokes the cat's brown, striped fur. She kneads my leg with her forepaws, nudges her head against my arm and purrs her appreciation in a sonorous contralto. I first saw her in an RSPCA shelter. A pathetic two-month-old bundle of fur who'd been abandoned with her three litter mates. With true feline artifice she made sure I did not leave without her. That was twelve years ago. Twelve is old age for a cat.

I scoop Marjorie from my lap, turn off the CD, wipe dust from a dust-free surface and rearrange some books on a shelf.

For you there may be children, grandchildren. For me – that cavern of solitude yawns again as I make the aimless rearrangement of the books. To grow old, alone. It makes me think of a crab retreating into its shell and never emerging again. I scold myself for being maudlin. I am not yet fifty. But living as I do, how will I ever meet someone else?

Some of the books tumble from the shelf with a fluttering thud. Marjorie runs from the room and I stoop to pick them up. As I start to put them back I see the small china tabby cat, curled up asleep, tail wrapped around itself. I pick it up, stroking it with my thumb, almost as if it were real. The first present you ever brought me. You found it in a charity shop and said you had to get it for me because it looked like Marjorie. I hid it on this shelf after you left; it was just too painful to see. And I am crying, sobbing as I have not done for months. Tears of regret, loss and maybe some self-pity.

Caro warned me not to get involved with a married woman. But we do not choose who we will love and I loved you. (Despite the neon warning signs that scream 'STOP!' at any woman contemplating such a relationship.) I hope you loved me too. That those words at least were not a lie, not just the expected, uttered like a form of lover's etiquette. I believe you did love me. You just lacked that particular kind of courage women who live 'my kind of life' must have. I pull a tissue from my pocket, wipe my face. I have to let go. I cannot live my life looking backwards, regretting. I never want to become bitter. Surely I will meet someone else?

I hope for this.

There is the sound of voices in the garden. They have arrived. And before I can go to meet them Stevie comes in, reaching out to hug me in her usual impulsive manner.

'We nearly missed the train,' she announces, laughing, 'and you will never believe why – Marcus, our punctuality queen, was late. Really!'

'Marcus, late? I hope you have evidence or nobody will believe you.'

And I go into the kitchen to put the pasta on. The china cat is still in my hand. I hesitate then drop it into the bin on top of wilted lettuce leaves, onion peelings and an old bread wrapper.

Her On the Water
Elizabeth Reeder

Rebecca:

She stands quiet feet submerged. She is all stillness. She
waits for me to pass by and into her arms but I have on long
trousers and do not like to get my feet wet.

Her bare toes play with water-smoothed stones,
concentrated hands expectant. She stands with her long
black hair flying wild in the wind. A calm look in her eyes.
If I do not go to her she may stand there all morning.
Instead of complying right away I linger near the rocks and
watch the divers do what they do best.

In between dives and re-emergences I watch her. Helen is
tall. So tall that when I first met her I wondered how I would
reach her lips for the first kiss. When I got closer I realised
that it was not simply her height that daunted me but how
she holds herself with a strength becoming a big woman like
Toni Morrison or a librarian I once knew. She commands
attention and I often like that because then I can take a back
seat. I can watch her in peace; I can let her be the brave one.

She wriggles her toes and the incoming tide makes eddies
around her ankles. She looks like she is not watching or
concentrating on anything but later she will be able to tell
me about all the birds that flew by or dived. She will
describe the sound of distant cars and how my breath
sounded a bit laden with summer asthma. She will tell me

about the smell of the leaves ageing and the steady odour of the sea.

She stands still in a way that I am not familiar with. I am slow, methodical but almost always moving. She alternates between rocksteady stillness and fast furious activity. In stillness she plans and processes; in activity she seeks knowledge and avoids reality. I plod on through and try to keep up. I often find that I cannot.

She lives life genuinely unsure of her next step and often changes her mind mid-stride. I can sometimes be confused about who I am living with. If you watch carefully you can see her change and change again. Her innate ability to hide herself makes her more vulnerable and ultimately a stronger person than myself. I sometimes feel as if I have wrapped myself around her and that she carries me through life.

She knows that I am watching her more than the birds. She turns slowly to face me and smiles. Opens her arms. As always my caution abandons me and I run shoes, trousers and everything through the shallow sea and into her arms. We embrace and dance in the water. Scare the divers and passing locals. We are two women in arms and the birds and the locals both know better than to challenge our exuberance.

Around and above me she stands mouth open to catch the rain. It falls lightly from high blue clouds. Water beads on her hair and rolls down. The water rocks her and snaps with quick drops. I have run back to the shelter of dry land, my anchor. Helen comes back too but slowly. Walking backwards she wills the tide to bring her a treasure. She treads carefully placing her toes first down along the spine to her heel. Resting and rocking. She comes back wet feet, empty-handed.

Helen:

Ice cold. After the first minutes submerged I can no longer feel my toes, my arches, my heels. My ankles become solid steel bracing up my legs. At first there is the pain of losing the sensation of something so important. Feet ground you, stand you in stead (good and bad), they support you, they spread out and give you leverage. If used right they can give you three more inches of height. They are peculiar and ugly in an individual way. My feet fit my body to a tee: solid, flat and perfectly proportioned. It's good for me to be without them for awhile. Without these occasional early morning sessions of stillness in salt water I'm not sure that I'd be able to stand as tall as I do.

Rebecca doesn't understand this but she never questions me or my unpredictable habits. She sits on the shore and takes in the scene. She wants to understand me but knows that she's missing something. She's whole. One. Singular. She's steady in ways that I could only dream of. What she was born knowing, she now knows absolutely. And although she might want to understand me, might want not to get her feet wet, she would never ask me to stop. She needs me to pull her and I need her to pull me back.

This pulling's never easy because I'm not one but many. I hear voices and while some disconcert me all echo and reply in stillness and unbearable reverberations against me. Predictable waves and unknowable patterns. Some I've named and others refuse to be pinned down to a single nameable form.

Some of my voices come in like storms: insistent and loud and I can argue with them, turn and face them. Let my anger, my anguish blow hot against their persistence. Others approach in silent and cunning ways and I'm at their mercy. When they give no warning I don't feel them coming and only feel their arrival by the unmistakable feel of breath blowing warm behind my ear. A mere whisper.

For a long time I thought that I might be mad. These voices urging me to run, to stand still as a heron, to take violence into the palm of my hand, frightened me and I wanted life to be simple. But life's not simple or straight-forward. I'm whole only as parts.

Standing in the tide the world is almost silent. Here, my

tallness shoots right up out of the water and my voices are silent. I'm no one in particular. I'm not even me and there's a peace in that.

Helen:

I hold him in the palm of my hand. His breathing, heavy, shortens. My fingers enclose his pulse, my palm forces his sleek blond hair into the pebble-dashed wall. He sweats with discomfort and I find this disgusting but keep pressing. Anger into palm, along into fingers and down into flesh. My nails dig ever so slightly. I'll not let him go bug-eyed but he doesn't know this. I'm transformed by his absolute disregard. Even here, my hand pressing against his neck, my knee sharp and bony pressed up and into his susceptible groin. He tries to pretend that it means nothing. I am, after all, just a woman.

My sister won't be happy but she'll be better off. I'd like to say that it is the first time that I have intimidated one of Anna's boyfriends. But it's not. Ostensibly I put them out because of big-man homophobic comments they make but really it's because she deserves better than these blond bastards whose skinny thighs are sucked into worn jeans. Because she deserves more than these so-called men who carry their violence like a wallet in their back pocket. Anna has had hand-shaped bruises and long strings of putdowns but took it as her lot. Secretly she appreciates my reactionary habits and wishes that she could use her six-foot frame in the same way. For some reason she feels compelled toward making herself smaller. Me, I'm on a mission to become even bigger.

He struggles now with the pain in his groin and the uneven surface beneath his skull. His eyes begin to see me as a true threat and he starts to feel the need for a good deep breath. A voice tempts me towards an extreme but I don't listen. I push him up and into the wall and then let him go.

He knows that he's lucky not to be beaten to a pulp.

We're standing outside Anna's house. I've already packed a bag with his clothes in it. He takes it and says nothing about the flannel shirt that I have procured for myself. I've donned it but plan to give it away. It's the gesture here and now that matters.

He walks down the path and wishes there had been a door to slam. In silence he came to visit my sister and in silence he has been made to go. It's odd that they know, being held by a woman like that, like a rag doll, that they just know better than to say a word. My hand pushes against their carotid, my knee against their pride and joy, but they are most afraid of my sweet baby blues whispering pure violence. Each of them have their own voices but here against a wall they listen to my Bella. Hers is the language of implied violence. I've found that sometimes, in times like these, it's the only language that they understand.

Peace flies on eagle's wings. I hold it, hold him, in the palm of my hand.

Rebecca:

She shoves him up against the wall of her sister'ís house. He clenches and unclenches his bony fists without effect. She has a good six inches on him and cares a lot more about her sister than he does. I say nothing and watch the scene, leaning casually on the car. She will not hurt him but he does not know it and that is why she is so effective. It is here, like this, that I feel her the most distant from me and closest to who might lie at her centre. Here she is louder and bigger. One voice moves her to act, the one loudest Helen; she calls her Bella.

Her back is relaxed and calm like she does this every day. But she does not. Not very many people in her life have ever deserved this. This skinny bastard does.

Righteous and right she has truth and physical strength on her side and I am thrilled to be her lover. She is unafraid and bold and one very small step away from being out of control. He crumples and she knows that she has won. Bella releases Helen and the neanderthal at the same time. He slinks down the path and growls in my direction. I smile and nod, give a small wave. Sensing Helen behind him he walks in the opposite direction.

Helen goes inside the house and leaves Anna a note. I have no idea what she will say but it will be short, to the point and unapologetic.

Rebecca:

Our feet pound on wet pavement. The sound of soles smacking is loud. We hold hands. Which feels like strength even though it is this small act; this tiny public acknowledgement of private commitment which means that we are running, being given chase in the first place. I am pulling her because she wants to turn and fight. I am running and pulling because I can feel my lips tingling; I will be no good to her in a fight. I strain and hear the five men chasing us (or are they boys, Jack the lads?). My jaw tenses and relaxes as we reach the corner pub. We push through the doors. It is a pub where we are known, it is safe.

We walk to the bar, the woman behind nods and says the usual. I feel giddy, giggly. My lips go wild when she kisses me and I hope that it will settle. The lads pound through behind us. The bouncers, clocking it all, ban their way and see them safely out of the pub and down the street. Pure dumb luck to be near a gay pub.

Jackie places the full cool glasses before us. This is the last thing I remember of the evening. The world goes dark.

Helen:

I see her swoon and catch her as she falls. The pub is busy but people open out to let me through. Get off the couch so

I can lay her down. My hands are shaking. She's warned me that this might happen. Should have known it with the giggles; so unlike her. I put my jacket beneath her head and rumble through her pockets to find her insulin. Jackie, the woman behind the bar, helps divert attention while I pull down her trousers and jab her hip. I hate needles and only know how to do this because she forced me to watch, learn and do. For moments like these. I didn't think that it would scare me as much as it does. She's out for the count: was there and then swooning. And not over me.

I saw myself turning. Letting go of her hand and facing the running men. I've never hit anyone before but I wanted so badly to feel their breaking flesh beneath my fist. Like somehow that would make a difference.

But I didn't turn, I kept hold of her hand and let myself be pulled. She was stronger than me, ran with a surer foot.

I realise as I hold the pen-like needle and carefully push the insulin into her vein that I am whole. There are no other voices. It's all me, Helen. Bella and the rest are silenced.

Rebecca comes to and I'm the one shaking.

She pulls me towards her, strong arms outreached and then pressed around me. For slow minutes, unfathomably long seconds, I hear her breath, feel her lashes butterflies blinking.

Helen:

I blink and it's forgotten. I open my eyes and it's remembered. I'm reminded. When I blinked his face disappeared. It was odd that such a simple gesture could obscure so much. It was a joy the blinking. It was the looking that was more problematic. In between times I couldn't make him go. He was still there looking innocent. Well respected. It didn't matter that he talked rubbish and grabbed me roughly and in the wrong places. No, people thought about how clean and well-pressed his suit, how tall his stature. How honest his lines of age. I looked, I squinted and still couldn't see it all.

He looked down on me, held me down. The flying made that better. I could watch like in a movie convinced that it wasn't me but a body double. An exact match. Ten fingers, ten toes, two hands, slowly blinking eyes.

Helen:

The cleanest break comes in the evening when my last meeting finishes, when I turn off my computer and the papers lie neatly piled: in, out and in process. My feet begin to itch in her neat black shoes.

My hands on the brass handle of the door signals a release. I step through the marble door frame, the big glass door and she's gone. My conscience, Ms Efficiency. As I walk to the bus I feel the shoes pinch, feel my stride inhibited by the skirt. She's asleep, buggered off until the next day at the office. She's as exact in her arrival and her departure as she is precise on the job.

She leaves me and takes my memory with her. I can only recall vague general details: clients, meetings, obligations, my first appointment in the morning. But she never lets me remember my successes. They are hers alone. I've never named her; we don't have that kind of relationship. Unlike the other voices she is unwavering and reliable. She also refuses to compromise. Nine to five are her hours, her clothes, her agendas and I'm a success because she is cut-throat throughout the day and I, Helen, am only partially there.

The loss of memory and the disassociation makes her the hardest to deal with. She comes in, takes over and leaves me no choice. I can look in the mirror and recognise the body but not the emotion that motivates me to put on lipstick or that makes the adrenaline rush faster as I close a deal. And although she seems to come and go at the doors of the office there is the sway time between home and the office where I'm not particularly capable or present.

Out of all the voices I wish that I could talk to her. Convince her to stay. I've this feeling that she is a bit of a tyrant and that she could rule the others. Her word could be law and her voice the loudest, calmest and most believable. I've tried to stay in the office after hours and force her into conversation but I always get caught up in work, win another client, get another bonus.

Sometimes I think that she plays tricks on me. Letting me remember, making me forget. It infuriates me and hurts Rebecca. I can't even apologise because the gap of knowledge is too big. Rebecca tries so hard to accept me, let it all run over her like water. But what can she do when this woman who looks like me, walks like me and talks like me cannot remember her name? Against the odds, she loves her and picks up her clothes after a long day's work.

Rebecca:

She slides the meticulous toe of one shoe into the heel of the other as she fumbles for her keys. Then she uses her shoeless toes to do the same to the other foot. Left first then right. Clicks and twists keys into descending locks. She picks up her shoes with one hand, holds her Versace jacket in the other, her shirt already pulled free from the waistband of her grey pinstriped skirt. She pushes the door open with her foot and, as she steps through, she drops her shoes, bag and keys onto the floor and hangs her jacket on a hook. Her hands go round to the back of her skirt and it slides to the floor as she steps out of it, along the hall and into the bathroom.

Tights, pants, shirt and bra, a trail along the floor to the shower. She is mindless. She washes off the day and settles back into herself. I follow behind her and pick up her clothes because she never remembers that they are hers. This is the weirdest part of our life together. Possibly because it is the most regular and the most unbelievable.

At first I could not understand why she could never remember what she had done at work when she got home. Why she would not always recognise my voice when I phoned her at the office. Why she would mumble about meetings and the sound of rain on the windows, but forget the finer points: the awards, the promotions, her success.

If I loved her I needed to know her. If I was to love her I wanted to understand how she worked. So I followed her to work, watched her over her lunch breaks.

I watched carefully for a few days that first year and began to notice how she walked differently, how her smile was tighter, professional. How she went into expensive shops and picked out really classy clothes. And developed a shoe fetish too. I was confused because the Helen I knew only ever felt comfortable in clothes that had known other owners, only wore trainers, boots or sandals. I wanted to demand an explanation but knew enough to see that maybe this other woman was an extreme of the ones I already knew.

I worry that one day this single constant in her life will be upset. That this voice will join the others or ask Helen to do things of which she is not capable. But for here and now she is fashionable, tidy and predictable.

Rebecca:

She has been running all day. She could not stop – the voices were too loud. They argued incessantly, rattling between her ribs. She refused to listen, she had heard it all before. They had nothing to say to her. Her grief was too much.

The funeral, the circumstances, the pomp had done her in. Her family would not speak to her. I stood at the back, her good friend. I watched how the family gathered together leaving an inconspicuous space between their entwined arms, tear-damp shoulders and Helen. She stood head down, crossed her arms. Stood with her legs wide, shoulders broad. Her height matching her father's, her brothers', her absent sister's.

Occasionally they pointed, became animated and apportioned blame in her direction. She watched the box being lowered and could not focus for all the racket going on inside.

She and I are the first ones to leave. She does not so much leave with me as walk beside me and then in the opposite direction. I take the car and go home. I recognise that there is nothing that I can do, nothing that she can do.

This was not meant to happen but there is inevitability in all things. Helen could not stop this any more than Anna or myself. I go home and look through old photographs, tidy the house. I do not cook because neither of us will eat. I have a bath and finally I give up the ghost and admit that I want her home, that I am tired of waiting.

She comes in sweaty and wild-eyed. She still wants space and I give it to her even though, for myself as much as for her, I want to hold her close. Share our grief, help to silence those that she cannot.

She stands in the dark of the bedroom. Small shadows of light flicker across her closed eyes. She does not sway but folds into my arms. She starts to come apart. I know, I understand and it is not enough.

Helen:

I stand in the dark and pretend to be asleep. They mumble on. They scream, they shout. Bella cries for revenge, others cry for suicide. Some yell for reason. I had walked and then run. I kept going and put my hand to my belly to make them stop.

I allow myself to be folded out of small flickers of light and down into the dark cool of the floor. They grow quieter. They seem to know that this will pass and I will still be here, that we will all survive. Rebecca whispers and cries. We've lost Anna and she says that it's not my fault. I try to get back the feeling of losing my quiet feet. She rocks us, unwavering in what she knows.

I'm torn. Anger rips through me. Powerless I watched on. The message had crackled on the old tape, her voice breaking with the routine of it all. The sound of the door being kicked. That bastard's voice in the background. I drove fast but thought that I had time; her door was strong and he was skinny.

It takes me ten minutes and I'm too late. His burly friend holds me back anyway with more than one too many enthusiastic punches to my stomach, to my jaw. I can't fight his bulk; Bella protests but goes quiet as he twists my arm. The skinny one has worked quickly. She lies like a rag doll and he had no qualms about making her go bug-eyed. He turns from her to me, smiles and walks through the door that his friend kicked in.

The big one twists and breathes heavily. It's then that I notice that Anna doesn't seem to be moving. I break free, punch giving skin and don't look back.

Her body lies at weird angles. Her face is pure pain. I phone for an ambulance. I don't know any of the good that I've ever done. She is all stillness. There is no peace in her and all I can do is hold her, hold her in the palm of my hand.

Out of Town

Chrissie McMahon

I was watching Abbey cook dinner in the kitchen of our apartment as the light faded outside the kitchen window. She does a sort of neat little dance around the room that is very, very cute. As I sat there, an admiring audience across the bench, I wondered at our difference. When I cook, it feels like a battle with aliens and nothing ever comes out hot at the same time. When she cooks, everything goes according to plan.

Abbey is beautiful. Everything she does has its own particular aesthetic logic and charm. She even looks good when she reads in bed, like before she went to sleep tonight, absorbed and attentive like a little, perfect girl. I tend to get greasy marks on the pages. She's just great, Abbey. She even has this cute face she makes when she...oh, never mind. I don't want to make her sound like any annoyingly perfect Ms Femme because she's not. She's real and she gets mad and spits and has cellulite and everything but she is just correct in an amazing amount of ways, that's all.

So, we're in the kitchen and I'm watching her and we are drinking wine and talking about some stories she is editing that are by 'emerging writers'. (I always balk slightly at that expression. It makes me think of water and shaking off drips and clinging to the edge of the bath. Awkward, blind scrambling is what it suggests to me, like something being chased up from a safe place under the earth.) I found it hard to concentrate on what she was saying. I was too busy watching her jostling the food around in the pan. It smelled exciting, that promising, oriental smell. I was wondering what it was, ginger and coriander or something. Lemon grass. She pounded it beneath the end of the knife and cut it up very small.

When I looked up she was frowning at me, poised like a Javanese puppet, waiting for my answer. I'm always asking her to repeat herself these days and it makes me nervous. Behind the bench my knee began to jiggle – up and down, up and down – like some old lady in a nursing home. I didn't notice it at the time. It's only now that these details come to mind, like advertisements or subtitles – appendages to the stream of recollection, distilled somehow and disturbing.

'So. Who was it – with you?' she asked, touching my hand.

I pulled myself together and quickly collected enough clues to work out what she was talking about.

'Shit. I don't know.'

I laughed. She blushed a little. We were quiet for a while. It was in that moment's silence, I think, that the kitchen became sort of desolate – the light outside had finished fading. The simmering food seemed sadly obvious and our cheer was gone. We lost our rhythm. I'm not sure why. But I rallied. I'm good at rallying and, okay, I panicked. What if we'd let the rhythm go altogether, if we allowed the dusky light to become gloom or left the food alone for once?

'It's a difficult question,' I said and I looked down again at my glass. 'Who was,' (and I *hated* bringing out the words) 'my first love?'

And I knew at the time that this was really cheating. I was exploiting an awkwardness that she always categorises to my advantage: Honest Woman Feels a Lot says Little. It gets me out of trouble but it is not the truth. The worst thing is – I know Abbey thinks she will help me to 'find the confidence' to speak about 'things' more naturally. In time. She looked at me across the bench with an expression of such intense understanding that I turned my face away. I went out then, to find some music. I put some folksy, dinner music in the CD player and that was when I started to remember.

It was cool under my parent's house. It was our place, beneath the floors of the house that I had lived in all my life so far. We used to smoke and talk and hang out down there all the time. Anne (who would have thought it was stupid for me to call her my best friend) and me, after school, Saturday mornings, Sunday nights. We were wild then – snaggle-toothed and bright-eyed. My parents gazed at us with bewilderment.

When Abbey asked me about love, in the kitchen tonight, with her complete and complacent understanding of the psychology of love – how it's a 'compendium of needs' and all that – this is what came rushing to just beneath my skin. Love?

I never saw any of the 'love' that I wanted on TV. I never saw it walking through the streets where I lived. In the darkening nights there were 'lovers' everywhere whispering and rustling, snapping elastic, swallowing alcohol and seeming to feed on each other's faces. This was not my thing. I knew it in my blood and bones as sure as anything. I walked like a ghost around the corners of the streets, around my house, listening to the sound of my own footsteps and the sound didn't frighten me at all.

Back in the kitchen, Abbey was singing along to the song I put on the stereo with a condescending, semi-humorous lilt, as though to prove she was not really committed to the melody or her performance. In the living room I squatted captive by the stereo, holding my wine glass, staring at my legs in their jeans, rubbing the denim under one finger, back and forward. I realised I was hiding. My memory hissed into a narrative, like a genie from a lamp. Abbey sang and clattered. I closed my eyes.

My legs were brown and scarred then and I went without shoes as often as I could, like every clichéd hick character you ever imagined. Anne and I practised kissing on each other in her bedroom with one eye sliding towards the mirror to see how we looked. French kissing was just weird and slimy and kind of disgusting at that point anyway. I remember feeling that it was like nothing so much as heated internal organs stuck in your mouth with a life of their own, fat and snaky. Even when we gave each other hickeys there was no sense of what was to happen between us. We used to shriek and shake with laughter; everything physical between us was a hilarious struggle. None of it was sensitive or controlled or awkward. It was all pure game.

These were dangerously absorbing reveries I was having, crouched by the stereo in disguise with my wine. I sat down on the carpet hugging my knees and pretended to be looking for music. The smell of food was everywhere. Abbey brought salad and utensils into the room and put them on the little low table which we eat at when we don't feel like sitting ghostly at the table by ourselves, 'making' conversation. I helped her to bring in the things and we sat. In the middle of the light of the fire I could clearly see her sleek head, her ponytail, the even lines of her sweater and her neck, the womanliness of her movements, her silver rings. I felt stirred, as I always do, when I take her in.

'So. Did you have a girlfriend when you were a kid?'

She asked me with her head to one side looking intent and amused at once. I didn't know what to say. I don't know why. I just felt – stupid, cross-legged and mute, on my cushion, with a mouthful of leaves and fish.

*

When Anne and I were first together it came from nowhere.
I had never thought about anything like that and neither
had she. It was dark, like I said, and we were under the
house and my mother was cooking some sort of disaster in
the kitchen. Some guy was on the radio talking about
snowflakes, I remember – on and on in a voice like a visiting
politician, the kind that makes you wonder what bogus
furniture would be in the house where this guy lives and
how it would be the sort of place where walls slid back and
mirrors reflected black and white patterns and everybody's
face would be red and smiling all the time. Anyway we were
lying on our backs looking at the beams that held my house
up when she started on about her mother.

Anne's mother was a nightmare of huge and disgusting
proportions. She used to beat Anne up any chance she could
get and then cry all over her the next day, saying that she
only hurt the people she loved the most. I never could work
out why she used the plural because as far as I knew there
was only Anne in her life except for the guys she brought
home. You could hear them in her bedroom through the
whole house like a bad joke – all times of the day and night.
It used to drive Anne crazy. I hated her mother too. I felt
everything Anne felt, her anger her sadness her madness and
her silence. The things she couldn't feel with me, like about
books or going to New York, she shut up about and that
was cool. There was no effort in our loyalty to each other.
We hated and loved and fought indiscriminately as a team.
It was easy.

I had never even thought of telling anybody how this was. I
guess I led most people to believe I was straight until I came
to the city.

For some reason I felt it was an important truth I must
now tell. We were at the table in the firelight, music playing
something mild in the background. On the lacquered
surface of the table, green and brown and golden plates and

leftover food lay between us like still life. There was no reason for me to feel angry.

'My best friend,' I said, smiling like an idiot. 'She lived around the corner from my house. Her name was Anne. We played basketball on the same team.'

Abbey was interested.

'You've never told me about her. When was it? What happened? Wait – wait till I get back.'

She picked up the plates and carried them out. I felt around for a way to tell the story. How to describe it at all? My imagination let me down. I was provided with no workable package. All I could do was recall.

So this day under the house we're just lying there and Anne started crying and swearing like a lunatic about how she had to get away from her mom once and for all. She knows she can stay at our place any time, even though my parents are a pain in the ass as well, don't get me wrong, but they're at least quiet during the night so you can dream undisturbed. But Anne is shaking her head and trembling like a little bird and she rolls over on to her stomach with her face in the dirt and she's really crying now and that's how it all started, I guess.

I just felt as though something crumbled inside me and I knew I had to touch her like I never had before. I held her hand in the dirt and she held mine back without looking at me, and out of nowhere I realised that I would never let anything bad happen to her. This made me feel good. The word 'love' came into my mind like a sign and, for the first time, I understood its power and its thrill.

I turned to Anne, lying down beside her in the dust under the house, and I pulled her chin out from under her. I kissed her on the mouth. Her face was damp and sort of messy and her mouth was swollen and she kissed me back. We tasted each other's mouths and chins and cheeks and eyelids. Then her hips were pressed against mine and I was trying to make them fit with me. Something was blazing in my blood. Between my legs was hot and damp and Anne was making noises that sounded prehistoric.

After a while, we were both grazed and panting and our faces were salty with her tears or mine or both. We looked at each other right in the eyes. There was something in that look that was like trying to tame an animal and it created a hard swallowing feeling in my throat. Anne was still and it meant we were 'there', just as though someone had said the word. We both heard it, I know that because I saw the movement in her eyes and she bit her lip. Suddenly, I was more afraid that this would end than I ever had been of anything in my life – of teachers or fathers or the baseball bats swinging out of car windows in the streets late at night. Of the love I never wanted, of giant and frightening creatures in the closet, of the nightmares of loneliness and strangeness that I had just begun to have, of the gigantic men who fucked Anne's mother, of Public Humiliation, of the guy on the radio, of well-designed interiors, of my dreams.

'Under my parents' house,' I said, too loudly.

Abbey came back in with more wine and she lay down on the sofa with her socks on. 'What?'

'That's where we had sex, the first time, when I was about fifteen. Under the house. My parents'. Anne. The girl and I.'

I was going crazy getting the words out and I threw myself down next to Abbey on the sofa and hid from her eyes. 'Well. That's pretty cool,' she said, pulling out her hair and trying to look at me. 'Were your parents actually at home?'

'Yeah, I think so,' I said. I sounded sort of childishly tough, I think, and I was relieved because the conversation was becoming flirtatious and we are good at subtle sexual banter. 'I don't remember it very well.'

'No?'

'Oh, it was probably after school or something. Summer.

I can't remember the details. It was pretty uncoordinated stuff.'

I was holding onto Abbey by now and I swear I was sweating like a maniac, on the sofa, her tiny compact body was in my arms and between my legs. I was sitting behind her, her head resting on my chest. Her hair moved through my fingers.

'But what was it *like*?'

And in a second, with a great feeling of despair and nakedness, I realised that it was no good. The whole thing was impossible to describe, in this room to this woman. I was afraid. It would come out wrong. It would all end up in a very saleable anthology. 'I don't know, Abbey, honey,' I said, very quietly. 'I really can't remember.'

That weird, scary silence again.

'Come on,' she said, and I could hear that she had given up. 'Let's go to bed.'

And so here we are. Hours later, and I am still awake. Rigid; my mind doing all kinds of exercises. Our bed is big and white and clean. There are books both sides and we look out of a large window at the cornices on the apartment building across the street. We sleep naked. We put our books down and turn out the light and we always hold each other, at least to begin with. Abbey sleeps soundly as though she is happy with her lot and she probably is. Tonight I look at her head on my breast and am struck again by how perfectly beautiful this tableau that she has created is. I try to breathe so as not to wake her. I try to sleep.

I grabbed Anne and held her and my body burned and she kissed me then and put her hand between my legs. When she touched me it was so good I put my fingers inside her. It was soft, I remember; touching her was like some kind of wet silk whispering. When I moved my hand within her she moved her hips and breathed hard and close to my ear. All the blood in my body was between my legs and my head rolled back and forward. She was moving around and murmuring and her leg was between mine, her hand on me, her fingers moving, her mouth in my neck and it went on and on. I looked down at her thin brown arm, and her hand resting on me and moving with grace and surety, and it was the most beautiful thing I had ever seen. I tasted the blood beneath her skin and the dust and a shaking went through me like the wind out of town, more and more and more and I felt her move to me, and her heart beat faster and faster, and she whispered words that were a spell in my ear and stiffened and shook and trembled and there was never anything like it in all the world, at that moment, the corny radio and the old, stupid books, parents' footsteps overhead, the doors slamming in the street, beams looming overhead and Anne's eyelashes on her cheek, her head on my collarbone, her dirty feet twitching between mine.

But now I am here. No longer afraid of my dreams or interior design or the smooth, neutral voices on the radio, which are still suggestive of comfortable sitting rooms. I am now often heard to say that I seem to have stopped even noticing the lovers who were so sinister to me before I found Anne under my parents' house. My secret is that I don't believe entirely in my safety or courage or in the supposed peace that this confident blindness has given me. I suspect myself of cowardice. I live with perfect Abbey in a safer, shinier place where trees grow in wrought-iron cages and I wonder what sort of courage it takes to be who I am, or if it takes any at all. Abbey stirs and I let her go, she turns in her sleep away from me.

Of course the back door banged like an old gun sometime after this and time had not stopped. And Anne and I put our clothes back on so fast we hurt ourselves doing it and ripped some stuff up as well. I saw her wipe her shaking hand on the front of her jeans and I did the same but I didn't want to and I wish I hadn't. I didn't look in her eyes for the longest time after that. I felt like a furtive animal.

When I toss like a crazy woman in our bed, and I often do, Abbey wakes me and holds me and we are two women in the night together between fresh sheets in a beautiful room in an exciting city, where lights and stars abound in mutual patterns in smug appreciation of each other's brilliance. Her hands are smooth and they do me good in the middle of the night. We are miles away from my home and I am who I am. I feel no dust beneath me, no panicky doors slam nearby when we make love but sometimes I do think of Anne and how she still goes by the sinister lovers on the corners of those streets, how she walks by their menace, long limbed and strong, brown and sour. She walks with all the sad ugliness of my town in a cloud around her. I know she does. I'm sure she does.

When I did look in her eyes, for the first time after that time under the house when we had both heard the word 'lesbian' and ignored it, gone past it, together, when I did look at her again, her eyes were clear and blank and proud. They called everything out of the corners and into the light. We were fifteen years old.

From that afternoon on we were lovers in secret for three years, with all kinds of different songs and sounds in the background. In cars and under stairways, in churches and our bedrooms with the windows open, at school and beside the road when we were far enough out of town. She was a brave wild girl and she never said very much. My parents asked me to leave when they found out about it all – and I did. Anne stayed. When we said goodbye she kissed me in the street outside the bus station. Loitering couples bristled and pretended to laugh at us and then I got on the bus. When I looked back she was standing in the road with her arms crossed and the words 'lonely as a cloud' came to me and I cried all the way to the city.

This is all long ago and so far behind me. I, I remind myself, am lying miles and miles away from the place where this all happened. I have made it. I am here, where I always wanted to be, with Abbey's immaculate head lying just above my beating heart. I struggle to put everything in its place within my mind. Something deep and lonely got started tonight with the idea of 'love' being raised in the kitchen. How strange. I fall asleep and despite my efforts to stay safely in the present, of course, finally, I dream.

Cool and bold and sweaty, we move in faded dusty places. Snowflakes fall on burnt grass and a wind that will never blow through me any more stirs the trees along a familiar road, and I wake up longing for desolation and terrible distant creaking and lonely radios – and for fire and love to take place courageously where it did, in the way that it did – when it was hard, when I was afraid and nothing was ever said or explained. When everything was real. When I was far enough, out of town.

Tzimmes
Tisa Bryant

a) Loosely translated from Yiddish, tzimmes is a stew of vegetables or fruits cooked slowly over very low heat.

Bon Appetit

b) The overcomplication of a relatively simple situation; a state of confusion.

The American Heritage Dictionary of the English Language

The route well established, this concerns both the missing grains and those that clump together.

1.

Her empty cup. Because it is no longer full, what remains is thought to be untouchable but yet must somehow be reached. Bow your head over the (scar, plate, memory or phantom feeling). The impressions are named to represent and hold. Silver platter. (Re)searching. A friend's religion. At the age when one should annually. Place breast on cold press, Olive. Pilgrimage. The light shoots through, darkens the overripe. Pot luck. Fate leaning over to serve it up.

A tight top. Domestic décolletage. Stay there and STAY THERE.

From hardwood to kitchen floor, I pace, peeking in the fridge. Is this chilling. Back to the map. Sticking pins in names, a spell to affect place and time, the shape of the land a butterfly in profile, or, as uncle likes to say, a pork chop. I of course disagree, more with the chop than with the pork. Heading west. Back to the bed, the breast. Sugar burns, explodes beneath the surface, into puffs, into blood, out of economy. Blood quickens. Early detection. Garnet yams, not jewel. This cinema, this research, this recipe. What is called for confuses.

She speaks directly, directing.

Place matzo meal, eggs, pareve margarine, apricots, ground ginger and apple juice on the auction block. And don't forget, pure cane sugar. Food soldiers against forgetting, packs a wallop, mounds, pounds, Mapp Hill. Grazing again through plantation names. Getting the picture. What went in to make us.

The Original Lists
OF
PERSONS OF QUALITY;
EMIGRANTS; RELIGIOUS EXILES; POLITICAL REBELS
SERVING MEN SOLD FOR A TERM OF YEARS;
APPRENTICES
CHILDREN STOLEN; MAIDENS PRESSED; AND
OTHERS
WHO WENT FROM GREAT BRITAIN TO THE
AMERICAN PLANTATIONS
1600–1700
WITH THEIR AGES, THE LOCALITIES WHERE THEY
FORMERLY LIVED
IN THE MOTHER COUNTRY,
THE NAMES OF THE SHIPS IN WHICH THEY
EMBARKED,
AND OTHER INTERESTING PARTICULARS

(unnumbered)

The type shrinks as it approaches the less and less desirable, diminishes in relation to the significance of the subject or place. What was left out is now untouchable yet must be reached. Some things do not appear at all. Some numbers emboldened, stand-ins for flesh. Cooking magazine. Haggadah. Pebbly, sticky stains, utensils resting too near paper. Evidence. Topography. Décolletage. What would cause the parish register to fuse together, then peeled apart, the print of one transfer to the other? Only one of those emboldened, a number deemed 'Christian' is (re)named. Hagar.

Every April, *Bon Appetit* has a Passover spread. Twists on old favourites. Make it new! What is called for confuses. The Four Cups, the matzos properly stacked and placed. The making of the afikomen. I insert other bodies, experiences, place them neatly on the table.

Midway through the first short, she enters. I whisper her to me. Doris boxes. She sleeps with Mildred. Leading lovers most absent from most movies. A breast shot would not be gratuitous here, but there is none. Murder and MURDER. The lights go up. I see few as young as myself. Concerns both the missing. Suddenly the awareness of my perpetual state of daughter weighs in. Their speech begins in the lower registers, the gravity seat. I am at once made relatively light and significant. After I leave she talks of all the women who. Remembering new and finally returning hair. The woman left her husband outside the frame.

On a ship bearing the family name thirty-three Jews from Portugal arrived with seventy-eight slaves in Barbados, on a ship bearing the seed of cane and hard labour sustained by empty calories. Negroes with names like '1'. The mother's heart bore Tituba up the Orinoco. Arawak women made good domestics. Like the ones in the picture. In tight tops. The secret is in the stuffing, the lightness struck through. Mildred sits back, satisfied. A good woman, that Doris.

No more inquiries here, but just in case, keep separate. You may need to make something of it later.

With blazing fingers, squeeze masses of steaming orange flesh from skins. Mix with unleavened meal and the cracked opened remains of unfinished lives. Add a little sweetener, and sanctioned oil product. My body stands attentive, watching the spinning mindless machine fight to blend the resistant masses. The meal like tiny fists, white blood cells. An occasional spatula pokes around the new body. Is this how it should feel? Ask her, all those hers. Who.

No mo' lasses here. We're so thin now.

The recipe, unsure of process and product. What is unmade can be made again. Visit the place of ingredients. There's no one to call for advice. Mummy's a Pro test ant. Pro distant. She's never been to the island. 'The Jewes' of St Michael had a separate listing in the parish register, but their blacks were also only numbered. Tradition, what's the difference? Who knows what lingers, mingles circa 1680, in the far recesses of the body. Who ever heard of a sweet potato matzo ball? My pacing yields no answers.

4.

Set ten large eggs on the counter. That was their number. Great grandmother, a middle child, bundling her daughters, hurtled towards the ship. Process with salt and ginger. He done wrong, was already too dark, the one she chose. He chose another of her kin. 'She came to me in a dream and bid me do evil.' Her father, the legendary Papi, salty, loaded his shotgun, held it low, not gingerly, and circled his quarry through the yard. The family luck. Yams are common on this island, and running men. The former generally has lighter flesh. For the latter it doesn't matter. Papi Cutting broke the compound down the middle; an imaginot line split the house. The sisters hid it from us, the house, but not the dividing blade, which we children chewed silently along its edge.

The house projects a regal decay. From it, melodies strain, springs through the four-poster carcass, the dissolving floor. What happens after excision, this. Ask

Mildred, boldly listening, perpetually about to hear. There was once a piano. There all kinds of cuts; all women know intimately at least one.

This branch has no leaves. Those men there are dead of death. And those, of circumstances not beyond their control, or so the women arrivants said. This research, microfiche. They come into view slowly, en masse a modest range rising above the island's midriff, somber Mt Hillaby, staring daguerreotypes, dates of birth. My eyes follow theirs to St Michael parish, unnamed veins running through it to the hills, the big house where they once stood over the city, the ploughed fields, the sea beyond. I stick a pin. There and THERE.

5.

The left panel of her tuxedo has been cut away, revealing the missing breast. This is what radical looks like. Her lenses glow. She recites statistics of women who, throughout recent ages, have. Phantom glandular pain and lineage. Take your lumps. Fat clouds drift above palm trees and jewel sea. They say that kind of thing skips a generation, Mummy said. I found such hope malicious, as I was 'next'. A row of flying fish caught on a line, flapping above the current, all riding the whip of the one up front.

After being brought, the men left with other women, or died. The left women left and kept leaving. She left her husband for a woman, as a left breast left or took leave, leave taking.

'And he went down into Egypt, and sojourned there…' What is your Egypt?' The disease of the child-free, manless, over thirty. Hot kitchen of the USA. Silence. Black Barbadian ancestors: Nonie first mother. Rosetta second mother. Edna and Elise the daughters. On a ship from Portugal, in 1680, named Jews with un-named slaves: Hester Nov with one. Rebecah Barruch with two. Ask her, ask all those hers and their hims, where they came from, what they brought, lost, or denied. What was let loose when the deck dropped. Egypt. From the breadbox I remove lots and lots.

A seasoned pro, got the hang of it, speedy expert fingers kneading, needing to make everything perfect, like the ones in the picture to find nothing like the one in the picture. The one in the picture, expressionless, hanging over the stainless sink behind the doctor's head, arrows indicating the slow circular motion of the hand (on a child's head, while sponging a pot, doing a gleeful Charleston, smoothing sand-castles by the shore, finding a stone, tossing it out). There is no next frame where everything breaks after close examination. The family name would be Cutting.

6.

Rinse suds well, wring hands. A neckbone of a problem. Give thanks and it will not break you, this lumpen batter and battered body, bless it, hold your head up. The bounty pressed onto the metal plate, seen through to the bone, this circular ritual. It should have been enough, but it wasn't.

She's known many women who have dealt with it, she tells me on the phone. She still has on her bow tie. I've always had a problem with my sign being that of a deadly illness. Once there was a woman who polled a room filled with women, asking for zodiac signs. When those under mine raised their hand, she gave her condolences. I haven't known any who have. Other malignancies, sure, to be excised, taxed.

Our director looks ready for a fancy party. She is wearing an altered tux. Her strong suit. Part removed. Seder and SEDER, she says, her finger pointing to the cast, the order of appearance for tasteful things. Action! Who ever heard of, but yams are common there. Keep palms wet to shape the balls. A compound of hills. The old man was a softstone cutter. Built the homestead, blood from his fingers in the coral mortar. And again, tonight, before the first wine cup, each will wash her neighbours' hands as lips release old ones from memory, from There.

7.

The family women were all seamstresses. They liked the word 'bodice'. They made their own aprons, stirred their own sauce. A stitch of water is a current, a vessel of history to speak from. Lives of Performers. Tituba wasted in Salem, by the book. 'As we hold this cup of wine, we remember our sisters in the land of —————who fearlessly stood up to—————.'

A film's central characters must have issues. The colours are bright and so are they, wisdom without sunset, for a time. Doris and Mildred run and play and then she gets the news. In the far distance breadfruit trees sway. One drops a ripeness that can be curried, but that recipe is lost. Doris is stunned. Down below, in the kitchen Great Gram hated a philanderer. She couldn't kill him, so she cut and ran to the mainland. Mildred stands at attention, awaiting orders. How to act. That one, with the missing breast, directs, sets sail, staff at the ready, sharp on top, daughter, assistant, weapon. Bloodlines course, edited through heredity, sex, to the next frame. Picture us, without blame. That one, directing, points a finger towards the mound on the horizon. If 'it' skips a generation, where does it land? My heavy state of daughter weighs in.

'Another food is haroseth, a thick mixture of wine, chopped fruits and nuts, meant to resemble the mortar used by the slaves to build Pharoah's monuments.'

What do we eat to ritually remember what we can only, and can't really, imagine? Pig feet and intestines go without saying specifically 'history', not kosher.

8.

Low and cool, the stove, the back door opens onto the garden yard. She bid me do evil. I have seen the mountain top. Spectral evidence. The wash house gavel drops skirts, issues forth a dribble of children and directives. There's a bright strain, a light streak running through us. Mildred arrives with bags of cheap clothes. Doris loves her anyway. Between them a space will be razed. As a child I wished to convert, have a draydel, the chore of Hebrew school and the next day's gossip. On the ship doesn't mean of the ship. This cannot be owned. It belongs to. 'Do you have any history of————————————?'

She speaks very quickly. The lenses of her glasses are thick. There is a young woman around, about, buoyant against the presented odds. The doctor's office is off-white with pale blue chairs. They all are. None soothe. She seems to burst. Hi, I'm Yvonne Rainer. Sign in please. We'll take your weight in a moment.

9.

She was mean, that Great Gram, favoured neither of her two girls, but favoured one for sport. Bitter herbs signify the harshness of ———————————. He done wrong; there was a third that wasn't hers. The only son died young. Thus the flavour the daughters absorbed, fought each other while defended what they were made of, breadfruit and flying fish, the blood in the mortar, the house they were born in.

Lifelines blur under water. They blur and they stutter. Falter. Lopsided halter. The wife. The knife in saucer. She cooks like a bride. The still from the film is sweet, sidelong, their naked shoulders, one rising up behind the other to whisper. Haggadah for healing. The four questions of the Seder change, are added to, subtracted. Can this lump be taken away without blood? Pierce with a fork. Cut in half. Scoop out enough to measure. Cool. Process. Why me? Transfer. Why you? Cover. Let stand.

The family tree. Islands. Mapp Hill. Lumps. Haynes Hill. Dropped seed. Cutting Road. Bitter fruit. Too much sugar in the system makes for a sour taste.

The wine raised in your names tonight will help me place or return to you. Stake a faulty claim, a distant identity. The careenage is full of houseboats. Deduct mystery conjoined to skin. Chill. Passover. They arrive and are last to leave.

10.

Sandwiched in the hold aboard the *Amitie*, the *Francis*, the unrisen, the bitter, (in)digested.

The bounty pressed onto the metal plate. An impression for each type. Inscription, prescriptive. It is written. You have. You must. There is a ribbon for this, as for. Tied together, they make.

Slapping back and forth. A ball like flesh like mud games and how Eve was fashioned slapped between hands a borrowed bone, roasted egg bitter herbs might cure a poisoned gram of mammary. What's another scar? Scream gentlemen, from your tuxes, this transparent audacity so suited to your luxury, cut through stitch by stitch, to reveal the makings of other territories. Two women, leading lovers, Mildred and Doris. This film director, her mastectomy scar, joins them, in her party jacket. The left panel of it is missing. Beneath is an iridescent lawn of skin, sustenance and pleasure razed. The family name would be a subtraction of parts.

Backgrounder, or A Place of Ingredients

Barbados is a hilly coral island in the Caribbean, the easternmost of the Leeward Islands. It is nowhere near Jamaica, but is close to South America. It is believed that at the right time one can feel the *harmattan* on the island, the dry dusty wind that blows from the Sahara and sweeps along the northwestern coast of Africa. The word *harmattan* is related to the Arabic *harem*.

> *I saw Barbados a limestone ham*
> *with a Hillaby frill on top*
> *Eleven saints slice it up*
> *and the English gulp it all down*

Chronicle of the Seven Sorrows, Patrick Chamoiseau

This is the place where my mother's family comes from. It is also the place where the Caribbean's first synagogue was erected, in Bridgetown, the capital of the island.

Tituba has been recorded by historians as having been either an Arawak woman brought forcibly up the Orinoco River, or an African of unknown origin, enslaved in Barbados. In Elaine G Breslaw's *Tituba, Reluctant Witch of Salem*, it is made clear that Arawak women were sought after as domestics by British slavers. After being handed over to the Puritan Samuel Parris and brought to the village of Salem, Massachusetts, and because of various mishaps involving deprived Puritan children, the healing arts and the art of storytelling, Tituba was tried, imprisoned for witchcraft, was later set free and then 'disappeared'. She has a supporting role in Arthur Miller's *The Crucible*, and uses Maryse Condé's *I Tituba, Black Witch of Salem* as a medium through which to avenge herself, correct her history.

Yvonne Rainer is a former dancer, choreographer, a founder of the Judson Dance Company in New York, breast cancer survivor, and the acclaimed director of several non-standard independent films, including *Lives of Performers*, and *A Film About A Woman Who*. *Murder and MURDER* is her most recent film, in which she appeared when least expected, looking quite dapper. The lead characters of the film are the lovers Doris and Mildred, who, with Rainer, mix it up with the stuff of life.

The Seder is an annual ritual meal during Passover that commemorates the end of Jewish enslavement under the Pharaohs, and their subsequent exodus from Egypt. The Haggadah is a sacred book in which the story of the deliverance is retold and is part of the process of acknowledging the sense of displacement experienced by so many people from many cultural backgrounds all over the world. *Haggadah for Healing* is a traditional/contemporary assemblage of instructions, prayer, songs, poems and anecdotes referred to in this text. The Seder plate is a large round platter pressed with hollows to hold the foods eaten in a specific order throughout the Seder, which proceeds in fifteen motions.

Seder comes from the Hebrew *sedher*, meaning 'order' or 'arrangement'.

The Original Lists of Persons of Quality, John Camden Hotten, London, Empire State Book Co, New York, 1874

Walk: Don't Walk
Sophie Smith

I have learnt how one must sail the stormy seas of attachment before one can arrive at the land of love. I have come to a place of greater safety.

Touch unearths feeling.

Healing touch disconnects me from time and space. It sets my mind free from its moorings and sends my ego downstream. It liberates words from behind closed eyes. I am a free spirit, an artist, a visionary. Touch anchors me, comforts me, smoothes my ruffled feathers, my wingbones, my broken-hearted spine. I pay to be touched.

I touched a woman once. I touched her with love and revealed her to herself. She touched me without love and revealed me to myself. I have paid for being touched. I have paid the price.

I became ill, a spiritual traffic light flashing WALK: DON'T WALK, in the form of ME. And I came out. Rudderless, broken and confined to bed. But free at last. Free at last.

Pain seized me like a different kind of lover. It gave me a before and after. I lay in bed. I set sail and watched the unwanted cargo of my life detach itself and float away. That is how the letting go happened. I watched as the tough canvas of its sail, carrying the maker's number, became smaller and smaller, a small white handkerchief, a faceless stamp, a speck of white, part of the blue.

Thinking was the first casualty of pain; it was too

strait-laced for that anarchist of the body. Pain threw thinking overboard and in the moments where pain was not, I found great plains of peace, prairies of peace.

I stayed in bed and read books. I read a page a day. Books with pictures. My bed drifted upstream with a following wind. I read a page a day. Books about healing, travel and Mother Julian of Norwich.

In the laboratory of my sickbed, great truths have been tested and proven. About faith. About hope. My world has become simple, sane, now all I have left is the day I stand up in.

I have come out of the blue and emerged into the sunlight of an identity, a fully formed lesbian woman at the age of thirty-seven.

I live in a row of terraced workmen's cottages in North Oxford. A psychotherapist and three musicians separate my house from Gabriel's. Gabriel is a lesbian of fifty. She teaches a life-drawing class and feeds the musicians' cats when the musicians are on tour. The street is quiet save for the sound of wind chimes, arpeggios and the occasional tearful wail or angry outburst from the psychotherapist's. We are all linked by the canal that runs past our gardens. Barges make their way slowly up the canal during the day, sometimes mooring for the night. We watch the walkers on the towpath opposite. We say good morning to the men on the boats.

Gabriel is doing a massage course and needs people to practise on before she takes her exam. I make an appointment.

I have not formally met Gabriel as I have only recently moved to my new house away from the hurly-burly of London but I have heard about her from the psychotherapist, Alice, who attends Gabriel's life-drawing class. I have heard about Gabriel's habit of pouring very large gins to unsuspecting guests and about the painting holidays in Greece that she organises once a year and which Alice describes as both magical and hilarious. Alice shows me the photographs from the previous one: women in batik wraparounds sitting on harbour walls with their water-colours and sketch pads; the same women, looking brown and showered, at long evening tables, taken with bright flash bulbs; Gabriel emerging from the turquoise blue sea.

I have also heard of Gabriel's kindness to strangers and those in need. The musicians hold her in high esteem for her 'chats' from which there are no wails or angry outbursts reported. They speak of her unsentimental wisdom, her cool approach and her surprising knowledge of musical theory.

I am surprised by how different Gabriel's house is to mine. The walls of my rooms are made safe with the warmth of books; I am cradled in the embrace of words I love and trust. Gabriel, on the other hand, has knocked down all the adjoining walls in her house to let in maximum space and light. The sitting room is dominated by two huge unframed canvases of women nudes. A series of water-colours of Greek churches fills the hall. In her study, where the massage is to take place, there is only one painting, a small eighteenth-century watercolour of Lake Geneva in a thick gold frame and framed photographs of Gabriel with her arms affectionately around different women. Large art books fill an entire bookshelf at one end of the room. At the other, a bureau faces the window which looks on to the long, narrow garden and the canal.

I have seen Gabriel row past my house sometimes but she seems taller in her own surroundings and more serious away from her fun-filled mythology, here to help me. She takes down my story on little white cards.

I look at how her short grey hair ends in an upturned wave along the shoreline of her neck. I look at the cracked spines of the esoteric blue Penguins on the bookshelf next to her. I look at her deep-set blue eyes, sheltered and full of experience, unequivocal.

I describe the symptoms of ME, the everywhere kind of pain, the feeling of being poisoned, the fatigue. I tell her the story of Rosanna:

Rosanna had been a close friend when we started our affair. I was still dithering about my sexuality and used to have long conversations about it with Rosanna, who identified herself as heterosexual but had strong sexual fantasies about women. She was keen to have the experience without the relationship. She said women were beautiful. She said she loved women but would not want that 'lifestyle'. What she wanted was a husband and children and all that went with them. Yet, when we had our conversations on these subjects, Rosanna asked more and more frequently in mock despair whether she would ever find a woman to sleep with. 'What about me?' I heard myself saying one evening half-jokingly, almost hypothetically, and with those words everything changed.

Our affair started with a kiss that was meant to go no further. We surprised ourselves with our compatibility, the power of our attraction. It was overwhelming. After years of friendship we had discovered the lover in each other and it was intoxicating. Surprise is a powerful aphrodisiac. At the same time, however, we agreed this was not a good idea, it would ruin our friendship, and drew up elaborate treaties to that end; suppers would not end in kissing. For the first few suppers we would meet full of resolution, only to yield with increasing delinquency by the end. The feeling of inevitability was unspoken but unmistakable. Rosanna went on holiday and on her return we made love.

From there the real trouble started. I fell in love. Rosanna did not. She could not afford to fall in love. She was playing a dangerous game with herself, pitting the lesbian in her heart against the heterosexual in her head.

Rosanna's best defence against sex becoming love was to blow up any bridges within which might make the connection. In the event, any bridges that were blown up were mine, those which connected the pathways of health. I was unable to let go. I was afraid to let go. I was unable to see any more. Love slunk away, no longer recognising its part in this story. When we made love, Rosanna would panic immediately afterwards and leave, barely having time to put on her clothes. Inhabiting increasingly different emotional zones, our friendship slowly crumbled. Power had entered where love should have been. My vulnerability and Rosanna's panicked anger in reaction to it grew in equal measure. We parted eventually, blown apart by our different expectations, hostile and diminished, no longer lovers, unable to be friends. Rosanna went to work abroad. We severed all contact.

Gabriel distils this story to the space of a white card.

'I have not been touched since then. Do you understand how important it is that I trust you?'

Gabriel nods. I have met an appointment with myself in coming here. I feel at home with myself in her presence, at home with her.

'Right, let's give you a massage. I shall be very gentle and I'm going to use lavender oil. Is that all right?'

'Yes.'

I go into the bathroom and take off my clothes. I look at Gabriel's toothbrush in its glass, the arm of a crumpled pink shirt hanging from the overflowing laundry basket, a silver cross on a chain next to the soap dish, a row of stripy knickers on the radiator. There is something upbeat and fun which coincides with the calm of these surroundings. I know I am in the right place.

I lie on the massage table and Gabriel covers me with a long white towel. She rests her hands on my wingbones and does not move them away. I can feel the healing warmth through the towel. She removes the towel to my bottom and pours oil into the palm of her hand. I am chatting while she does this but the first touch of her hands stops me in mid-sentence, made silent by the sudden sacredness of the gesture which mainlines itself via my skin to a place without words. The branches of the trees outside rustle into the silence. I follow every nuance of Gabriel's fingertips as she massages my back and my shoulders, slowly, in rhythmic waves – effleurage, effleurage, effleurage. Her hands are strong, competent, unsentimental. My mind attaches itself to her wrists like a spinnaker catching a sea breeze. She sails my mind on to open seas, the open seas of the spirit.

After a while, I hear her voice asking me to turn over on to my back. She holds the towel above me as I go about and covers my waist and breasts, leaving the shoulders and chest free. We laugh at the awkwardness of this manoeuvre.

'Are you all right?' she asks.

'Yes. You have a gift for this, it's wonderful.'

'Thank you. I love doing it.'

Then the silence again. As Gabriel places her fingertips just below my collarbone, near to my heart, I am brought forcibly in to the present moment and it overwhelms me. My body wants to break open with tenderness but what my body does is freeze. My mind is filled with love, my body with fear. All sensation leaves my skin and I can no longer feel Gabriel's touch. My back is quite numb and I cannot move my legs. I am a frozen body with an underground stream of hot tears coursing through me. My body closes as my heart opens. The love in the present has released the love of my past; love for Rosanna whom I loved so much, love for myself whom I did not love enough. Gabriel has removed her hands at the sight of my distress and stands at my side in silence.

'What am I doing wrong?' I ask without knowing where this question has come from.

'Nothing and you are not being punished by being ill.'

'I can't feel anything.'

'This happens sometimes. You are distressed.'

A private voice never used comes from me. A child's voice. 'This is who I am.'

'I understand pain, Sarah.'

'I am not allowed to be afraid.' Again I use words I have not consciously chosen.

'You haven't been allowed to feel anything. It is hard to be lesbian sometimes. You are realising the power of feelings suppressed. Rigidity can make people ill, thinking there is only one way to do things, to look at things, to be.'

'I hold in a lot.'

'I used to do the same. I have suffered. I understand.'

'But you are happy now?'

'Yes.'

'I have a strange feeling that in some way your happiness guarantees my own.'

'We are all linked. People are extremely precious to me.'

'Thank you.'

'I am here to help. I'm going to end the massage now. How are you feeling?'

'Still a bit numb, but okay.'

'Take your time.'

I have remained lying down while we speak, comforted by Gabriel's voice. I am shaken by this wave of emotion, ambushed by its force.

When I am dressed, Gabriel makes a pot of tea. We sit opposite one another in deep chairs in her studio, a room filled with light, empty save for rags and canvases and paint. Gabriel has a stillness in the way she sits and speaks which is at the same time relaxed and energised. I feel I can ask her questions and she will answer.

'I feel I have all this creativity and I don't know how to get it out. I want to write but I don't know what to write about or how to express myself.'

'Paragraph by paragraph, that is how it's done. No one just writes a novel. Go home today, sit down and let an image or feeling or twenty minutes that changed your life come into your mind. Then let another one and write it down, then another. That is how I paint, stroke by stroke. We paint and write on our scars. You know about unrequited love. Write about it.'

'Like everyone else does.'

'Like you do. I will read it. I was once a postulant nun but I left before I took my vows because I was in love with the Mother Superior.'

I burst out laughing. I almost fall off my chair in surprise and delight.

'Really?' I ask three times, too dumbfounded to be more coherent.

Gabriel laughs too. 'Oh yes, it's hard to believe but it's true. It was some time ago and since then I have returned to the art training I received at the Slade, as you know.'

'The Mother Superior?'

'The Mother Superior.'

'That is extraordinary. Did she know?'

'Oh, yes, she knows but she is a very wise woman and in a way she saved me from a life to which I would never have been suited. The Church still has a very negative attitude to homosexuality although things have started to change, slowly. I felt very strongly called to serve Christ, however, and I still do, but in a different way now.'

Images of the Greek painting holidays return to my mind. I smile. 'Does Alice know?'

'Oh, yes. I am quite open to talking about it, where appropriate.'

'You are amazing.'

'I am not amazing. It would be arrogant of me to say I can identify with your pain if I did not identify with my own brokenness. Brokenness is part of our humanity, the part we must embrace, that small voice in you which said "This is who I am."'

'Do you still love the Mother Superior?'

'Yes, but it is different now. One does not have to give up

anything or anyone. You have to give up the attachment, that's all and then you can really love.'

'Is it that easy?'

'It's not that difficult.'

'What do you mean by attachment anyway?'

'The false belief that without a certain person or thing or belief one cannot be happy.'

'How do you do it then?'

'By learning how to see.'

'Like a painter?'

'Yes.'

'I don't know any other lesbians.'

'You do now.'

It is lunchtime and fatigue is knocking at the door. Luckily, I have only to walk past three doors to get home. Gabriel shakes my hand and as we stand on the threshold of her house, her parting word is 'rest'.

In the months that follow, I write paragraphs. I sit at a table overlooking the canal and wait as images surface in my mind. I start by writing one paragraph a day, then two, then three. My little minnows of images grow into large shoals, moving inexorably in the direction of a story. I feel I have conquered the world.

During this time, I continue to lie on Gabriel's massage table once a week. We exchange childhoods, middle years, recent histories, previous addresses, favourite writers and painters, turning points and Achilles' heels. Gabriel's life, though different in its details, seems to resonate into my own story. I do not feel alone. I ask questions. She gives answers. And intermittent to the touch, I hear the beat of wings.

This morning, I am sitting on the bench at the end of the garden. It is a beautiful July day. In my lap is a letter from Rosanna. After two years of silence, words. Quiet and clear, whole-hearted. She remembers the years of our friendship before it all went wrong. She makes no attempt to defend her behaviour. She expresses her deep regret. She will understand if I do not wish to respond.

Her words return me to the ocean-deep sound of the Rosanna I have always known. I know their genuine affection; I can taste it. Now, as I sit quite still, the paper weighted by my hands, I can feel my heart opening, very slowly, like a big, pink blossom. Peace enters in the shape of gratitude. I look at the water in the canal. A duck does a somersault.

A little way off, I can see Gabriel approaching in her rowing boat.

'I passed my exam!' she calls up, lifting her oars and allowing the boat to take its own course for a moment.

'That's wonderful!' I call back.

As she continues downstream, she shouts behind her, 'Thank you! Come round this evening for a drink!'

Gabriel has passed her exam. And I have passed mine.

And Baby Makes Four
Shamim Sarif

1. The Girlfriend

There is a restaurant in Paris that we go to, very occasionally. I was surprised when she took me there first – it was not the ornate, stiff place, filled with Michelin stars and impossibly rich food that I had expected. She knew all those places, of course, and there were many she admired, and remembered, and liked. But this place she really loved. It surprised me because I didn't know her or the restaurant so well then, but in fact they found in each other almost a reflection. The place was expensive, but understated; elegant, but not formal; passionate and yet consistent. It was run by a mother and daughter who were warm and expressive and who filled the place with character. And the food – the food was the freshest, most delicate, and most sensual that I had ever tasted.

We sit across from each other, and while we wait for our starters, we spread pieces of warm, fresh toast with home-made soft cheese, and eat them with marinated olives, a pot of new-churned butter and whole basil leaves.

Hanan looks at me and smiles. 'You like the champagne?' she asks.

'It's wonderful.'

'Good. We're celebrating.'

Expansive and generous by nature, she has never in our lives waited for a celebration to order champagne, but I am eager to find out the reason.

'I think it's time,' she says, her black eyes dancing, her tongue pausing, as always, too lightly on the letter 't', giving her words that seductive Middle Eastern accent that I associate with starry desert skies, and rosewater-scented sweets. I am looking at her blankly.

'I said, I think it's time,' she repeats, a little more slowly.

She means the baby. The champagne bubbles explode in my stomach, and quickly I eat a piece of bread. We have discussed this over the last three years, of course, and I know that she has always planned to have a child at a certain age. But that age had seemed years away, and then it was months away; and after that whenever we talked about it, I was happy in a vague kind of way, and I wondered how I'd really feel when the time came. Now I know.

'Have you stopped breathing?' she asks.

I can see lines of concern on her forehead. I shake my head, and try to look reassuring. Inhale, exhale. Breathing. Easy. Anyone can do it.

'Why now?' I ask, in a voice that sounds as though I've been gulping helium.

'I'm thirty-six,' she says. 'It was what we discussed.'

'I'm only twenty-nine,' I reply.

That doesn't change her age at all, but I say it again, plaintively, as though it might.

'But we discussed it,' she says, reasonably. 'It will be fine. It will be wonderful.'

'You say that about everything,' I mutter.

She tosses her curly head, smiles a disarming smile, and shrugs. 'And have I ever been wrong?'

Logic. It'll get you every time.

2. Her Husband

We already know who the father will be. Another irrepressible optimist, so that between the three of us, the proverbial glass will always be two-thirds full. By profession he is a surgeon, a philosopher and also a successful artist.

'Good genes,' Hanan had said.

And a good man too. Honest, kind and excited about everything. He tends to view Hanan as a goddess of mythic proportions, who has benevolently descended to earth to allow him to father her child. He is sure the baby will be unlike any other the world has seen, a kind of new messiah, but not a religious one of course; a philosophical one.

'I told him my family were originally from Bethlehem,' Hanan told me. 'Maybe that set him off.'

As yet, he knows little about Hanan's personal life, except that she has been engaged five times, which Hanan herself considers to be a little exaggerated, even by her generous standards, but which Karl takes as a completely creditable comment on her character. He also has a vague understanding that she is forever being pursued by eligible Arab men, all of whom have the unstinting approval of her parents. So he agrees to meet her mother and father after Hanan has broken the news about her intended pregnancy. They decide on an Indian restaurant for lunch, and as her father watches Karl, ominously snapping poppadums between his fingers, her mother fires questions at him:

'Are you Arab?'

'Yes. Well, Egyptian.'

'Good, good. Christian?'

'I was born Christian,' Karl replies, heroically stepping back from the philosophical arguments rising in his mind.

'When will you get married?'

Hanan sips at her salty lassi. 'Mama, I already told you. He's *gay*.'

Mama promptly commences a fit of tearful coughing of such ferocity and volume that it brings the entire room to a standstill.

'Too much chilli?' Hanan ventures.

Her mother fixes her with a mournful stare that makes it clear the masala chicken is not to blame. The poppadums lie in crumbs beneath her father's hands.

The meal lasts rather longer than planned, but to Hanan's surprise and gratitude her parents are not threatening, or unkind, just disconcerted and uncertain of how to proceed.

'They come from the Middle East, after all,' she tells me later. 'And they're a different generation.'

So it is agreed, and Hanan marries Karl. An appeasing marriage, but a strong one, for it is understood that the basis is respect and trust and liking.

But Karl still knows nothing about us.

We go to meet him for lunch. He sits across the table, smiling, and perspiring, happy and slightly off balance. His eyes are dark from a night spent painting, before seeing patients in his morning surgery.

'I'm so excited about the baby,' he offers, moving forwards in his seat.

'Karl, before we talk about that, I have something to tell you,' Hanan says.

He sits back and wipes at his forehead with a napkin.

'I'm in love,' Hanan tells him.

'Oh, God,' he says, and I'm sure he is about to cry. 'I'm so happy for you, darling, really I am. Even though you're my wife. *Especially* because you're my wife. I want you to be happy. But you do know he might not let you be in charge, like I would. Middle Eastern men . . . '

'It's not an Arab,' she says. 'And it's not a man.'

He looks at me, registering. 'You mean . . . ?'

We nod.

'Yeeeeeessssss!' he shouts.

Everyone in the café looks at us. It occurs to me that perhaps we should start to stay away from restaurants.

'We are going to be the world's best family,' Karl says. 'And now I have two wives instead of one! I love you both! And I love our baby!'

3. His Mother

We decide against turkey baster-style efforts at impregnation. I am willing to give it a try, but even as I try to convince Hanan my hands keep shaking. I think this puts her off.

'What about a fertility clinic?' Hanan asks.

'Which one of you is infertile?' I reply.

'Mmmm. True.'

Karl knows a woman whose gynaecologist did the job for her. This seems a sound idea, until everyone remembers that Hanan's gynaecologist is Karl's mother. It was how they had met many years ago.

'But Mum would be thrilled,' Karl assures us. 'She doesn't practise much any more; after all, she's seventy, but I'm sure she'd be delighted.'

Hanan looks at me. Exhale, inhale, keep breathing. I am grinning like a Hallowe'en pumpkin.

But Karl's optimism is well-founded, or perhaps it creates and spreads its own good energy to his mother, for she is, in fact, delighted; after all, it means a grandchild that she had never expected. When she walks Hanan upstairs to her office, in that strong, practical face are a pair of eyes that carry a sense of wistfulness, of possibilities missed in her own life. She fought an eastern upbringing and a traditional husband to forge a career as a doctor, and a very fine one at that, but many emotions – for her husband, and even her sons, had often been lost along the way. But she is happy now, if a little bemused, at this new way of doing things. There is none of the bitterness that I have seen some other women of her generation show; she has no wish to wreck the present to make amends for a past spent fighting. So she orders her syringes, dispenses advice, and carefully counts the days, waiting like a mother hen for eggs to start dropping.

4. The In-laws

And did I mention that my parents are Muslim? They know that I am with Hanan; I told them early on. Giddy with joy, I fortuitously remembered my mother telling me that all she wanted in life was for her daughters to be happy.

'But, Mum, I'm so happy,' I told her after breaking the news, but I wasn't sure she could hear me through her sobbing. I waited awkwardly for her to stop blowing her nose, but it took a while, and by the time she faced me, red-eyed and disappointed, I felt too sick to speak.

'And now I have to tell them about the baby,' I say to my sister.

'They're idiots,' she says, kindly.

'I know, but what shall I say?'

'Do you want me to tell them?' she offers. She loves telling people about her gay sister, her potentially pregnant girlfriend and the philosopher/artist daddy. She thinks the whole thing is very cool, and adds a certain cachet to her own life. 'It's like that film,' she says. 'You know – *The Cook, The Thief, His Wife and Her Lover.*'

'How?' I ask, exasperated.

'How what?'

'Never mind.'

5. A Walk in the Park

A few weeks later, we are out walking. It is a cool day, late spring, but softly damp here in the park. Rain-moist leaves drip heavily above us. Our pace is languid; I match my steps to hers, beat for beat, recalling the sound of her heart pulsing against my ear in the stillness of that morning's dawn, considering whether there would soon be another heart racing inside her.

She turns to me with a kiss that brushes my lips as gently as the rain. In her tangled curls I can smell the wet grass and leaves that are all about us. Her long, calm fingers take hold of mine, and place them over her stomach.

'He's already here,' she says simply. The world around us goes quiet and for a long moment, Time does not take another step.

6. Baby Talk

Six months later, and this baby boy, still ripening in the womb, has heard English, Arabic and French. Long strands of language, and oceans of music – Bach, Puccini, Cole Porter. Poetry and a little Shakespearean drama. A dissertation on Wittgenstein, and lots of nursery rhymes. We have exhausted all avenues of entertainment, and he hasn't even arrived yet.

We make an appointment with the obstetrician to discuss the young man's entry to the world. A residual heart murmur tips the balance in favour of a Caesarean, which pleases Hanan. She runs her own company, and there is a lot to do. She whips out her electronic organiser, while the doctor flips through a desk diary.

'It should be a week before you're actually due,' murmurs the doctor. Pages flip, and screens blink expectantly.

'Shall we say Thursday the twelfth?'

'Perfect!' says Hanan. 'That way I'll have the weekend to recover.'

The doctor laughs sweetly – what a good sense of humour, she is thinking to herself, but Karl and I know better. Her laughter trails off as she watches Hanan's uncomprehending face.

'It's a Caesarian,' she says firmly. 'Not a walk in the park. You will need your husband, and your friends' (a nodding glance at me) 'just to help you get out in seven days.'

'Seven days?' Hanan repeats, as though appealing a prison term.

'It may be reduced to five,' says the doctor 'But only for good behaviour.'

7. Is There a Doctor in the House?

Two days to go before the birth, and I am walking down a hospital corridor. I am tense, afraid, trying to be strong. The smell of bleach is making me feel sick.

I find Intensive Care and sign in. Karl is hooked up to several IVs, his leg is the size of a small dinghy, and he is reading Wittgenstein.

'Karl, how are you? What's wrong?'

He throws down his book. 'I'm so sorry. I didn't want to worry you.'

'I panicked when they phoned...'

'It's only a blood clot,' he says. 'I got cramps, I'm perfectly fine, I knew what it was...'

'What *was* it, exactly?'

He tries, and almost succeeds in finding a way to make the words 'heart attack' sound like 'sore throat'. A clotting disorder, just discovered. The clot in his leg means days, weeks or even months in hospital. He will definitely miss the birth.

'It's fine,' he tells me, because he always believes that everything is. 'You'll go in there, with Hanan, and it'll be the two of you together, watching our baby being brought into the world and it will be wonderful!'

After I leave, I realise that I have forgotten my scarf, so I return. The Wittgenstein is back in front of his eyes, but even from the door of the ICU, I can see Karl's hand coming up to brush away tears.

8. Raging Bull

My mother telephones in the afternoon. Breathes distress and misery down the receiver.

'What can I do for you?' I ask, curt, hurt by too many emotional slaps from those small, wringing hands. I have gone so many rounds sparring, encouraging, trying to help her understand, that now I am punch-drunk. In need of a rest.

'You know you're going to burn in hell?' The concerned, everyday voice, as if she has just phoned to warn that rain showers are expected later.

'At least it'll be hot,' I say. I put the phone down, take off my gloves and step out of the ring.

9. The Main Event

Thursday morning, 9 a.m. The epidural is in place, and we sit in a state of stunned excitement, stupefied, thrilled to think that in one hour's time, the two of us will be a threesome.

'Should I phone the office?' Hanan asks, only a half-joke, but the drugs are beginning to work, and she looks drowsy.

In the theatre lots of people in green oversuits stand about smiling. I get my own set of sterile clothes and a mask to wear. I've never worn a green v-neck before. It's a day for new experiences.

'Where's your husband?' asks the doctor.

'He had a heart attack the day before yesterday,' Hanan replies.

'Isn't it lucky you have such a good friend to fall back on?'

I smile and try and look solid and reliable, but the dialogue alone makes it feel like the set of a hospital soap opera. Someone switches on the radio, and 'Unchained Melody' is playing. I search for some hidden significance in this song playing at this moment, but I don't think there is any. The nurses are swapping news over the operating table.

'Going to Cornwall tomorrow.'

'I went there last year.'

'So did we. Every year I ask for Mauritius and we get bloody Cornwall.'

I don't even realise that they are already operating. I take

Hanan's hand and glance over the canvas screen that is stretched across her chest to block her view. I wish I hadn't. She can tell my smile is forced, my eyes panicked.

'It's only a tiny cut,' I tell her, lying.

And suddenly they are lowering the screen, and lifting her head, and our son is being pulled out. He arrives, his torso twisting upwards, hands outstretched to the light above, head flung back, suspended like a piece of breathtaking sculpture. He looks nothing like the crooked, crouched alien drawings that we followed month by month in the book. He is downy-haired, blood-covered, slimy, shiny-skinned and beautiful. And then he yells, a primeval scream from the depths of his lungs, and everyone laughs.

10. Love is Blind

They say that when you close your eyes, your hearing becomes sharper. This is not true, not right now, right here. I sit, quietly, listening. Behind my closed eyelids beats the searing red of sunlight, slanting through the window of Karl's hospital room. The longer I close my eyes and listen, the less I can hear. Perhaps it is a result of a month of too little sleep, perhaps just a conceit. But the steady, pulsing noise of the drip monitor fades. So do the sounds of people in the corridor outside – a nurse's laugh, an old man speaking too loudly. The idling engines in the parking lot below us have melted into the buzzing warmth of my sun-filled eyes.

All that is left behind is the sound of our baby, drinking, pulling slow draws of milk out of a bottle. His father is holding him, with gentle hands, and I can hear him murmuring a lullaby.

Something touches my finger. In this strange state of heightened drowsiness, I can follow my own reflexes, feel the ripple of my nerves telling my eyes to open and look. I resist, and keep them shut, waiting. I feel her long fingers entwining with mine, a hold that is delicate and strong at the same time. The sun on my eyes. The lullaby. And the murmur of the baby. A moment of grace, here, now, after the nappies, the bottles, the uncertainty, the wonder. I smile, and grasp her hand, and the sounds and the moment, and promise myself that I will never forget them, ever.

Hunting
Julie MacLusky

Hastings Excavation
c/o Novorossiysk Central Post Office
Black Sea Region of Krasnodar
Russia

17 October 1861

Dear Beth,

I know you must be desperate for news of John, and thus I am including a short letter with this package.

The enclosed Russian shawl contains some very delicate scrolls. I suggested that we hide them inside this parcel to you, to secure their safe delivery to England. Other artefacts mailed directly from this site to the British Museum never arrived. Make sure the scrolls go straight into the care of our friend Henry Johnston (head of the Classics department), at the British Museum. Tell him that under more agreeable circumstances, we would have enjoyed presenting them to him ourselves.

We are having a little trouble with the local people, and thought it prudent to get these artefacts safely away from the site. The scrolls had been hidden inside the organ pot (usually reserved for the heart, stomach, etc) of two female skeletons, which had been bound together and entombed well away from the main excavation.

The name of Hypolytta, the Amazon queen, is inscribed on the scrolls in both Greek and an unidentified language. Both bodies were holding small, well-worn bronze axes, with blades shaped like crescent moons, inlaid with silver symbols. The two silver earrings engraved with Amazon symbols are truly unique and may prove to be extremely valuable. Logically with two bodies I would have expected more jewellery – which, if we have time, we may find.

The two fair braids of hair are a little gruesome (it is rather horrible, the way hair survives as well as the bones) and mean these women were probably related to the 'White Scythians' who traditionally occupied this part of Russia.

This grave is not quite what we were hoping for, and a little out of my field. Greek mythology has Hypolytta eloping with Theseus, then dying at his side defending Athens against her tribeswomen. If this legend held any truth, her skeleton would be buried in Greece, and not hundreds of miles away on the far side of the Black Sea. Thus I think this is unlikely to be *the* Hypolytta; maybe it was a sacrifice to her, something of that sort? Only a proper translation of the scrolls will tell.

We are fairly confident now that this must have been a major settlement. The network of tombs have yielded at least a hundred female skeletons; whether they co-existed with the surrounding settlements, or fought them, remains to be seen. Homer, I think, described the Amazons as warrior priestesses of Artemis. I remember a very dull Classics teacher, Miss Heathdene, becoming quite animated as we worked through a passage of Herodotos, which described how these women formed their own fighting community when their men were slaughtered, rather than become the chattels of the enemy. A very extensive dig will be needed before any valid hypotheses can be drawn up. These tablets might help make the British Archaeological Society look more favourably on John's request for funds for an official excavation.

At the moment further progress on the dig is impossible. The locals seem to be blaming us for the failure of their crop. They believe this whole area to be cursed; John had to bribe the village elder dearly for access to the site. Unfortunately some of the younger staff have not shown much respect for local customs. Over the years I have learned this is the key to a successful excavation.

For several days the local people have been chanting to appease a sea goddess, who they believe is angered by the desecration of her land. Jeffries went to the market today and reports seeing many new faces. He suspects they are rabble-rousing bandits, who may exploit the villagers' fears to raid the site.

This letter goes with the expedition's guide, who sails for Istanbul to get help. My thoughts are with you and both the children. John sends his love and will write as soon as he is able.

With love from
Your sister-in-law, Katherine Hastings

Classics Dept
British Museum
Russell Square
London W1

15 February 2001

Dear Jenny,

Enclosed is a first draft of the Hastings fragments. Shame they got mothballed for so long – but the whole thing has always been taken for a clever Victorian hoax, more so as most experts believe that if the Amazons existed at all, they were from Northern Turkey.

The American mining company that came across the dig found it exactly as described in Katherine Hastings' letter.

The burial chambers had been stripped bare, but they have found significant female bones, together with about seven more recent male skeletons, which are probably the remains of poor Hastings' group. Katherine Hastings' fate remains unknown. She was the only woman on the expedition – she had managed to work, unofficially, on over fifteen digs. One of those Victorian women who became sick as soon as they returned to England, and spent every moment they could out of the country. A recent biography of nineteenth century archaeologists even argued that Katherine Hastings should have been given credit for some of her brother's discoveries.

As for the translation: even that wouldn't have been possible without the work done at Harvard by Deborah Stein and that clever new Russian scholar – another benefit of the Berlin Wall coming down, all these guys working for us.

I think it could be worth leaking a copy of this draft to the minister. Even at this stage, it might help our campaign against closure. Ironic that this supposedly mythical tribe of women could end up securing the future of the museum's research department.

Looking forward to seeing you at the Pre-History Conference in Athens. If you have any thoughts on all this before then, give me a call, x5549.

Sincerely,
Sue Lansdowne, Asst Curator, Ancient Collection

Sue Lansdowne, First Draft Translation of Hastings Fragments

Hyppolyta's Story: The traveller's news
Although the visitor was a stranger to me, he told the guards that he had news of my husband, Theseus; thus he was brought through to the terrace, where I spend most of my days, high above the sea.

As the stranger, Lysis, climbed the steps I thought he must be carrying a delicate singing wind chime as tribute; but when he bowed to me, I realised that his intricate jewellery was making the music. Lysis had a bare shaven face, as is the custom in Crete, and wore the fringed kilt and heavy jewellery loved by the Minoans. I knew then why Theseus had befriended this man.

Even though the Minotaur was long dead, Lysis would have reminded my husband of his own coming of age, in the Cretan Bull Court at Knossos.

The guards watched over us as the visitor, Lysis, told me how he had first met Theseus. They had both sailed as tribute on the last ship to supply King Minos of Crete with human sacrifices for the Bull Court. Later, Lysis had been among those Theseus led to safety, when he had killed the Minotaur, and called on the earth-shaker, Poseidon, to destroy the Labyrinth. Lysis had not settled well to his freedom. He was an adventurer, like many of those who had survived the acrobatic jousts held to torment the great bull of Knossos. After drifting from city to city, working as a charioteer, he had joined Theseus on his most recent expedition.

The light was fading to a greenish glow as Lysis' story ended. Staring out across the dust of Athens, towards the East, I could feel him watching me.

Then, too quietly, Lysis asked, 'Can you imagine a world where men are absent?'

Even after these years as Theseus' wife, his question made me laugh, and avoiding his eyes I wrapped my shawl tightly around me. He could not have seen my markings, but he would have heard Theseus tell stories of his tamed Amazon queen.

Lysis drew his chair a little closer, and said, 'In my land, the one who smiles at her own thoughts in company is honour bound to confess the matter.' I hoped my silence would encourage him to take his leave, but Lysis patiently awaited my answer. 'I survived in the Court of King Minos, where girls from your tribe made some of the best bull dancers. Now tell me, what made you smile?'

Lysis had pressed me too hard; afraid that the fever of remembrance would seize me, I left him with the guards, and retired to my room. At the household shrine, I made offerings to Persephone, praying that she could deliver me from the spirits of my past.

Night has fallen; the star you were named for has taken its place in the Pleiades above me. I thought to see you again, Maia, only in the Elysium, the abode of the blessed dead. The visitor has fooled me into naming the dead, and thus bringing the other half of my soul back to me. Until the fever passes, I shall remain here in my bedroom; I hope the visitor will be gone when I awake.

The Land Where Men Were Absent

We had been up hunting since dawn, and found nothing. Our horses slowed as the sun took up full power in the sky. The rasp of the crickets grew louder as all other sound was obliterated by the heat. Still we hunted, without speaking. We had been together so long that I did not need to see you to know where you were looking. Although I had not heard the hind in the scrub behind us, I halted my horse at the same time as yours, slid off carefully and tied them both up to a tree, without us needing to exchange a glance. I stepped through the dry grass after you and our forearms touched as we lay. Only then could I see the hind, which was sheltering under a tree, panting, and looking in our direction. Lifting my arm away as you drew back the bow to fire, I could already taste the roast meat, the good wine and the love we would be making that night.

We made quick work of the carcass, aware that we were farther from the city than we should be. We were riding hard, with a long way still to go, when the track turned sharply, and we found ourselves on the edge of a ravine.

That was when we heard the cry – a pained, human-sounding noise. Flattening ourselves against the earth, we crawled to the edge of the cliff.

On the steep slopes below us, we saw our first man.

This was the being whose armies had extinguished so many lives. This was the creature we had heard of only in battle songs over late campfires, when we were children, on those first communal hunting trips. We knew they were needed for child-making. Each year a few of our warriors would regain their fertility, by giving up training, before leaving to capture a man.

Of course I had seen the infant version in the city, before they were weaned and left out each year for the migrant tribe we allowed to pass through our lands. How strange that such a soft and perfect infant could develop into this peculiar adult form! Knowing some shame at its appearance, it had covered its body. It moved its ungainly limbs in such an odd way that our eyes met and we almost gave ourselves away with our laughter. It walked as though it had something uncomfortable between its legs, as though it had lost some essential part of itself, and was searching for it. Those thick limbs could not have been developed for any practical use, as they seemed to block its proper movement, and took away the grace that is the birthright of all earthbound creatures.

We were too dazed by the heat, we should have left – but entranced by the creature below, and safely upwind, we watched as a few more of its kind appeared. They seemed to be searching the ravine below for something, and calling to each other, using a primitive kind of tracking. As they drew near we began to realise our danger, and shrank back to leave. It was like tracking a wild boar and finding him suddenly upon you. For the first time I saw fear in your eyes, and fumbled with my horse's bridle, my fear feeding on yours. Our horses, sensing our terror, stumbled, and as we headed into the bush, gave us away with a terrible chorus of whinnying. The hunt began.

The capture and the beatings were the more painful for the dishonour in being hunted like the hind we had killed earlier.

We had been warned not to stray so far ever since we were children. When we set out on this, our last long hunting trip together before the initiation, the city elder had warned us, and she had foresight so we should have known. We should have known.

To give the savages their due, after the beating, on the sea voyage, they left us alone. They did not want to touch us while we were on the water. Maybe they believed it would make their gods angry? Once we reached their city, we were kept penned with the other livestock, while a stage was readied for the auction. Our captors seemed to be watching the harbour constantly, awaiting the arrival of a special ship.

I dreamed and dozed a lot in the daytime, and examined my limbs, grown soft. I was only alive because I knew we'd escape when the auction was over. They seemed to think we had been tamed by our capture, which gave us hope. My worst fear was that even when we did break free, we would not be able to find our way home – even the stars were different there.

I thought I should never get used to the sight of them, the way they sat on a horse was ridiculous. The animals must have been specially tamed to get used to such treatment.

Watching their strange behaviour at the marketplace helped the time pass. Their daily duties were divided between the men and women, and some adult women did the tasks of children in our city. There were no old women – at first I hoped this meant they were considered too wise and honourable to mix with the young. But later I realised they must have been killed, or cast out. Some of the wise ones in our city spoke of such things, but before seeing it I thought they were stories that had been twisted a little in the telling and retelling.

We were guarded and watched all night as we slept by the fire. I thought they'd like us to touch – a tale they would tell when warmed by wine, on their hunting trips. One night, curled up behind your back, I woke to catch one of them staring at me, very hard. I could not read his thoughts. They have odd manners; they stare into each other's eyes even if they are not lovers. They do not know how to avert their eyes.

This is what the guard wanted to know, I think, how we came to be bonded to each other, how it all began. That made me remember the first time I saw you, at court. You were full of anger, at your parents' decision to give you up as tribute to my strange tribe. As the rites of welcome were read to you, you wriggled free and for a moment I thought you would run. But you were only struggling against the indignity of being held down. As you went through the ceremony your brown eyes met mine.

I had such a strong image of your gaze that I was afraid I was looking at a ghost in the firelight. Then you turned in your sleep, and I felt your hand slide over my ribs, pulling me back, telling me we would soon escape.

The elders knew straight away, of course, and watched our friendship grow with good humour. I would have been terrified if I'd known what they could see, of what would happen, but I knew nothing except you, your voice, your face, your company.

Remember the day we were accepted for our initiate training together? By then it would have been impossible for us to hunt well if we were parted, but they had been known to separate lovers. The elder in charge of our initiation thought this last hunting trip would take the heat out of us. I wish it had. If our wits had been sharper, we would never have been caught.

I used to catch my breath just to be near enough to you, to see the pulse in your neck quicken, as you fitted an arrow to your bow. Our initiate mother warned against this passion. She said true hunters never lie in each other's arms after the sky begins to lighten.

At first we slept together as children do, because it was convenient as we were training together. I was used to the heat of you next to me, stroking my hair back, curved around me in sleep. When did it go further? Was it that time at the river, when we lay on a hot rock, in the shadows of the early evening?

We were just talking, I remember now, our faces close, and your pupils grew darker, until I couldn't concentrate on what I was saying, and my heart kicked against my throat, because it knew something was going to happen. I was a little scared, and talked quickly to hide it, and then your finger touched my lips, and you shut me up with a kiss. When the pressure of your arms around me lifted and you traced a line from my breast to my hip, I trembled with the charge from your touch. It took a long time to become accustomed to that.

The guard who was watching us could not have known, he was as far away from that as he was from the strange stars above us.

As I dozed I imagined the faces of our people, as we rode back in through the gates. I wouldn't allow myself to think the impossible, that we would stay. We'd get back in training, in the night, and as soon as we were sold to our new owners, we'd break free, and go home.

One morning as we woke there was more noise than usual; they babbled the name 'Theseus' over and over, and we realised that it must have been his ship they were waiting for. Theseus' gold would raise the heat at the auction, and increase the takings, as people would enjoy trying to outbid the great hero.

After Theseus had paid for us we made plans to escape. We had learned enough Greek by then to understand the sailors as they talked of the voyage ahead. As they brought us on board they argued about whether the ship should hug the land for as long as possible, or cut straight across the treacherous Cycladic sea, to Athens. The loudest speaker, the one who would oversee the ship's galley of slaves, said Theseus was losing his courage, and getting old, and would use the excuse of having a fully laden ship to take the more cautious route.

The first days onboard we were kept bound together, drugged, in the hold. One morning I woke shivering from cold, and realised that the bindings had been cut, and you had left me. They told me you had leapt overboard, trying to escape, and had drowned. I knew they lied, but could never find out what had happened. Much later, when Theseus was very drunk, he taunted me, and said he had had you killed and thrown overboard to prepare me to be his wife.

Once in Athens, I was fed well, given wine strengthened with opiates and brought to Theseus. As I fell pregnant quickly, my time with him was soon over. They kept me well guarded because they thought I might try to escape as soon as they had taken his infant from me.

Theseus is not evil. Since the birth of his son he has done me no harm. There have been some restrictions – he removed all the female slaves from court and replaced them with eunuchs, to try to teach me to be a Greek wife, his wife. He soon found he had wasted the gold he spent on my purchase.

My escape would not cause Theseus to mourn: he deserted Ariadne, who he led from the Labyrinth, before me, and there have been many others since. The injury would be only to his honour; for that alone he would think it worth sending out a hunting party to track me down and bring me back.

Since she was not with me, I decided that the palace was as good a place as any to await my own death.

As I woke from the fever, I felt Lysis' presence in my room. Before I could reach for the bell to call the guards, I felt his hand on my shoulder. He said quietly, 'She is alive. She made me promise to bring this message to you.' A guard walked past and he paid great compliments to the craft of my shawl, and removed it, as if to examine it; when he handed it back I could feel the package he had hidden there.

After sending the guards for coals, I unwrapped the package and found first a short silver curl of hair, bound in a metal comb, the kind we used only for our firstborn daughters. Next I uncovered a single silver earring. Its cold metal made me shiver as I held it up against its partner, which was still warm in my earlobe. Trembling I searched the wrapping cloth and found the last object: a tiny shell, which gave out only the faintest murmur of its home, a beach on the Euxine Sea. Lysis said, 'She is living in a cave overlooking the bay. I led a raiding party along the coast of Scythia; we were shipwrecked, and she saved me. I owe her my life. She nursed me back to health, and would take no reward, only that I should bring this message to you.'

'I do not understand why you would agree to risk your life to do this.' As I spoke I realised we would not have much longer – the guards had never before left me for so long with a stranger.

'There is a balance to be paid – twice women from your tribe have saved my life. Two girls from your tribe volunteered to take on the bull on the last day, in the Bull Court, on the day Theseus lead the rest of us to safety. One girl was gored – the other died trying to get her clear of the bull. Then Poseidon, the earth-shaker, brought down the palace, and buried their bodies, and all those of the Minoan Court who had come to watch the spectacle. If I had not brought this message, the Furies would have made me pay the balance with my life.'

'You have done your duty. But escape is impossible. I have no friends here.'

'The balance would not be paid by the message alone. I have brought my own gold, enough to bribe you a passage home.'

The guard had returned, and did not like us talking close. Before I had a chance to reply, Lysis rose, and told them he wished to retire to his room. As he left, he said, 'I sail in the morning. When I call to bid you farewell, I hope you will let me know your decision.'

The eastern stars which will guide me on my journey have now risen over the sea; it is time to quell the ache, and take the last voyage, home.

Contributors' Notes

Samantha Bakhurst was born in London in 1968. She has lived and taught in France, both in Nice and at Brittany University. She has also taught in London, where she has worked with Asian and Afro-Caribbean youth groups, producing documentaries, that explore the themes of racism and class. Samantha has worked as an arts project coordinator, managing projects such as the *Young Evening Standard* children's newspaper, the Eclectix Film and Animation Project and Architecture and the River. She now works as a writer and film-maker. She writes for educational textbooks, abridges books for Radio 4 and has edited *20:20 Magazine*. She writes short stories and is currently working on two novels. She is developing scripts for radio and television. She has produced and directed commercial and music videos, and educational programmes for the BBC. Samantha writes and directs independent films with Lea Morement. Their first award-winning short film *4 p.m.* was screened at Robert Redford's Sundance Film Festival in 2001. They have made a second short on super-8 mm called *Story of An Afternoon* and are to shoot their next short *Bubblegum* this year. They have nearly completed their first feature script.

Alix Baze is thirty-seven years old, born and raised in Cardiff. By nature, she is a traveller, and much of her adult life has been spent experiencing other countries, but she continues to return to Wales. Presently, Alix is studying towards a Ph.D. in Critical and Creative Writing at Cardiff University. During the first year of her doctorate the university employed her as a teacher of creative writing for undergraduates. Since then, she has been focussing on her own writing of poetry and short fiction. She feels strongly about the issues that face dual national, same-sex partnerships. Much of her work reflects this. She hopes her story 'Green Card' does a little to help raise awareness of the type of hurdles such relationships encounter. Alix has a Bachelor's degree in English Literature and a Master's in the Teaching and Practice of Creative Writing. Her ambition is to become a professional writer. 'Green Card' is the first story she decided to submit to a publishers and she is thrilled that it is appearing in this anthology.

Frances Bingham was born in 1961 in Northumberland and now lives in London with her partner Liz Mathews. They work together at the Whitechapel Pottery, where Liz is the studio potter and Frances runs the ceramics gallery. Her interest in music hall and theatrical cross-dressing started in 1983 when she took a degree in English and Theatre. A prize-winning poet, her long narrative poem *Mothertongue*, about the lives of women actors through the ages, including a music hall male impersonator, was published in 1999 as a limited edition artists' book, with images by Liz Mathews. Frances also writes non-fiction and is a regular contributor to *Diva* magazine, writing articles ranging from 'Drag Kings of the Music Hall' (1997) to 'Sylvia Townsend Warner and Valentine Ackland' (2001). Her short story 'Double Tongue' was published in the *Diva Book of Short Stories* (2000). Frances also performs her work, most recently at SpitLit, the women's literature festival (2001). She would like to dedicate 'The Recognition Scene' to Liz, with love.

Tisa Bryant was born in Tucson, Arizona, in 1966. She spent most of her adult life in and around Boston and Cambridge, Massachusetts where she was a seven-year member of the African American writers' collective, The Dark Room, before moving to San Francisco in 1995. She has conducted creative-writing workshops in elementary schools and colleges, and has worked as a curator for film programmes, panel discussions, and visual arts shows in collaboration with local community organisations and activist groups. Her work has recently appeared or is forthcoming in *Chain, Children of the Dream* (Pocket Books, 1999), *Beyond the Frontier* (Black Classics Press, 2002), *Hatred of Capitalism* (Semiotext(e), 2002), *POM2: Property of Many; shellac, Step Into A World: A Global Anthology of New Black Literature* (John Wiley & Sons, 2000), and *XCP: cross cultural poetics.* Her chapbook, *Tzimmes* (a+bend press, 2000) is available from Small Press Distribution, www.spdbooks.com. In addition to her part-time jobs as business manager and bookstore clerk, she is currently Lesbian Fiction Editor for *Blithe House Quarterly*, an on-line journal for Gay/Lesbian fiction, at www.blithe.com.

Julie Clare was born in Ipswich in 1963 to conservative, Caucasian, Catholic parents who trailed the family around various identical RAF camps from Cornwall to Morayshire. Fortunately she survived to tell a few tales and loves doing this in writing and performance. She lives mostly in a much maligned city in the north of England, where a successful teaching career enables her to satisfy her wanderlust and funds ambitious holiday schedules. Julie, aka 'Ms Pleasure', lives life to the full and enjoys singing and dancing, loving and holding, larking about and dreaming on, swimming and submerging, dressing up and undressing, walking up hills and running down them. She also spends time and energy on issues close to her heart, from feminism to human rights. Julie is lesbian to the core and believes this makes all the difference. She is currently exploring her butch side, though her friends claim not to have noticed.

Shameem Kabir was born in 1954 in London where she now lives. She identifies herself as an Asian lesbian feminist. She has a BA Honours in English and an MA in Women's Studies. She has been published as a reviewer of TV, music, film and books, and has written lyrics for television soundtracks. Hers was the title story of *In and Out of Time*, an anthology of lesbian feminist fiction published in 1990. She has also written essays for anthologies and is the author of *Daughters of Desire: Lesbian Representations in Film* (Cassell, 1998). She has worked in television and in women's publishing and now works freelance.

On issues of displacement and the need to belong, she is aware that home is more than a geographical location or geopolitical position. As an Asian living under white supremacism, as a woman operating within a phallocentric social order, as an out lesbian who is aware of entrenched homophobia, she knows home has to hold a sense of internal sanctuary as well as actual safety. Coming home has involved inhabiting a body not colonised by men, a body celebrating her lesbian identity.

Sophie Levy was born in North London in 1978. She survived suburban, conservative Judaism and a private girls' school to become a lesbian and a poet. She has been published in many zines and magazines including *Angel Underground*, *Entropy*, *vines* and *Siren* (Toronto's lesbian magazine) and been a *PoetryEtc*-featured poet. Her three years at Cambridge were spent editing the LesBiGay and Women's newsletters, the 2000 *Oxford and Cambridge May Anthologies of Poetry and Fiction*, writing the Edinburgh Fringe show *Kassandra*, part of which was aired on BBC Scotland, and winning the Kinsella/Ryan, Quiller-Couch and Bridport supplementary Poetry Prizes. She currently studies avante-garde women's writing for her Ph.D. in English Literature and Women's Studies at the University of Toronto by day and the Toronto lesbian scene by night, reading regularly at the dyke bar night, Clit Lit. She writes film reviews and the Sinema column for www.thecontext.com. Sophie has a book of poetry, *marsh fear/fen tiger*, forthcoming from Folio/Salt in 2002.

Mary Lowe was born in Bath in 1959 and lived there until the age of four when she moved (with parents and newly acquired sister) to London. Mary went to college in York then moved to Newcastle-Upon-Tyne, where she has lived and worked for the past fifteen years. Day jobs have included teaching, sexual-health training, psychiatric nursing and energy-efficiency training. She has had work published in *New Welsh Review* and *The Fruits of Labour* (The Women's Press) and her play for children, *Rap up the Planet*, was performed throughout the

North-east. She has an MA in Creative Writing from Northumbria University and she spends long hours stroking her iMac computer in the hope that one day it will produce a work of genius.

Chrissie McMahon was born Christine McMahon in London, 1969. Shortly after her birth, her parents returned to Australia and settled in the city of Melbourne, Victoria, where Chrissie attended high school before going on to study Arts and later a Dip Ed at the University of Melbourne. Chrissie began teaching in 1990 and continues to do so today. She began writing as early as she can remember and this is her first published story which deals directly with her sexuality. Chrissie currently divides her time between London and Australia and continues to write and teach.

Julie MacLusky is a writer of fiction and screenplays, living in Santa Monica, Southern California. She worked as a broadcast journalist in England before moving to California, where she is a Professor of Screenwriting at a major University. Two of her screenplays are in development, and her short stories have also been published in a certain Mammoth Collection.

Background to 'Hunting': The dig is based in the Krasnodar region on the North side of the Black Sea, which is the region described by Ancient Greeks as 'Scythia', which in legend is where the Amazons came from. There is no proof that Amazons existed outside mythology, although recent archaeological digs in Russia have uncovered numerous graves of 'warrior women' who are buried with their armour and sometimes horses. Currently Themiskyra in Northern Turkey is considered to have been the Amazon heartland. The story also borrows heavily from the legend of Theseus, as he married Hypolytta, queen of the Amazons, after defeating the minotaur.

Elizabeth Reeder grew up in the suburbs of Chicago, went to Kenyon College and moved to Scotland in 1994. She worked in a feminist organisation for six years until she took redundancy to focus on her writing in July 2000. She teaches writing in

Glasgow and for the Open College of the Arts. She loves vast open spaces.

Coming out was long and painful and, obviously, the best thing she has ever done: her writing improved tenfold when she could be honest. Her story, 'Crosswords', was short-listed for The Macallan/*Scotland on Sunday* prize and she has had other stories published in anthologies and magazines. By the time this book is published she will have finished her first novel and will be well into her second.

Elizabeth would like to thank ARTT, FM, her mom and dad for their love and support in her life and writing. Her goal is to be happy and inspiring and to live in the Northwest of Scotland and/or the Southwest of the United States.

Shamim Sarif was born and brought up in London. She is of Indian descent, although her parents and grandparents were born and raised in South Africa. The great richness and unfortunate limitations of this cultural background formed the inspiration for her debut novel, *The World Unseen*, published in May 2001. She studied literature at London University and Boston University, and began her writing career with the publication of a number of short stories in the USA. Shamim is an accomplished screenwriter, with three scripts under option in Hollywood, including that for *The World Unseen*. Acclaimed director Deepa Mehta is attached to direct the film.

Using writing to challenge people's perceptions is a primary aim of hers. When a reader identifies or sympathises with a character or situation they are usually more open to a change in thinking – which can only be a good thing.

Shamim is thirty-one and lives with her partner, who runs her own toiletries company, and their son in London. She is obsessive about food and cooking, and collects wine – slightly faster than she drinks it. She also loves music – particularly jazz – and plays the piano.

Rhiannon Satis was born in Hertfordshire in 1957 and grew up on a farm five miles from St Albans. She feels deeply her connection to her rural working-class background. Though education and life choices have taken her away from this, she still defines herself as working class and English because British smacks of colonialism, patriotism and empire. Rhiannon lives and works in Sheffield, Yorkshire, sharing her life with her partner and two dogs and four cats. She has on-going mental health problems and it was partly for this reason she recently gave up a stressful job in a government department. She now plans to work as a freelance writer and launch her own craft business.

This is Rhiannon's third publication. She has performed at Huddersfield Poetry Festival and various venues in Sheffield. Her work is due to appear in an anthology later this year with the Opening Line project, showcasing Yorkshire writers.

Rhiannon views her sexuality as part of the rich mix, making her who she is. She regards writing as one of the most subversive acts a body can engage in. She dedicates this story to Keith and Brenda, her second set of parents.

Sophie Smith was born in England in 1961 and grew up in London with her mother and two sisters. She received a Catholic education at More House School, an independent school for girls. She read English and American Literature with an option in Film Studies at Warwick University from 1980–3. Shortly after graduating she lived in Rome where she taught English as a foreign language and developed an enduring love for that city. On returning to England she worked in publishing and subsequently as a self-employed freelancer. She continues to live in London and is currently writing a novel. Coming to a full understanding of her identity as a woman has freed her to fully express herself as a writer. It has helped her find her voice both on and off the page. She finds writing a source of great joy and her vision of life is enriched by a lesbian perspective.

Cea Vulliamy is a lesbian feminist who was born in coastal Suffolk in 1973 and grew up in Hull. She has a mixed class background and doesn't fit neatly into lots of definitions, class or otherwise.

Having worked with various children and young people's projects and organisations, Cea has gone for a complete change of track and has trained as a reflexologist. She is loving not being in an office and being able to spend time in the garden which is much more exciting than working.

She currently lives in Wales, still by the sea, with her partner Anne, and Anne's lovely children, Phil and Sarah. Cea and Anne are nurturing dreams about a little place with a plot of land where they can create their own ecologically sound paradise with an organic garden and no neighbours.

Cea has had various pieces of poetry and a few short stories published in anthologies, and wants to write much more than she does but life has a bad habit of getting in the way.

Jocelyn Watson lives in London and is of a mixed racial heritage. Her mother is Indian (Goan) and her father is English (Geordie). She was born in Hong Kong as a result of which she speaks fluent Cantonese and Mandarin. Jocelyn has been active in feminist and Black politics all her life and, as a staunch internationalist and trade unionist, was the first Black lesbian to co-chair UNISON's National Lesbian and Gay Committee from 1999 until 2001. She studied law at Cambridge, is a qualified solicitor, and has been the Black Lesbian Caseworker for Lesbian and Gay Employment Rights (LAGER) since 1995. Jocelyn began writing in 1987, supported and encouraged by the Asian Women's Writers Collective. In her writing as well as in her political and personal life, she is committed to promoting the interests of all diverse and discriminated communities, not only in Britain, but throughout the world.